T0095352

Palace of the Pharaoh

A Marshall Mane Archaeology Adventure

Sequel to
THREE KINGS OF CASABLANCA AND STONE OF THE SAHARA

ROCK DILISIO

Editor
ERICA M. HOLLABAUGH

PALACE OF THE PHARAOH
A MARSHALL MANE ARCHAEOLOGY ADVENTURE

This is a work of fiction. All of the characters, names, incidents, organizations, and dialogue in this novel are either the products of the author's imagination or are used fictitiously.

iUniverse books may be ordered through booksellers or by contacting:

iUniverse
1663 Liberty Drive
Bloomington, IN 47403
www.iuniverse.com
1-800-Authors (1-800-288-4677)

ISBN: 978-1-4917-5513-6 (sc)
ISBN: 978-1-4917-5514-3 (e)

Printed in the United States of America.

iUniverse rev. date: 01/15/2015

CHAPTER 1

EGYPT – 1948

I PEERED AROUND THE CORNER of a rug seller's stucco building. A gust of wind greeted me with an exfoliating blast of sand. I felt as though I were a cat waiting in wide-eyed anticipation for its prey to cross its path. If I had a tail it would be gyrating with adrenaline. As heat waves bounced from the pavement as though choreographed, a mass of humanity swelled around me on this busy Cairo side street. The slow, almost defensive approach, of two, seemingly local men meant little to the throngs of people going about their daily lives. They were though, in fact, my targets. More specifically, my quarry was carried in a satchel slung over the shoulder of the taller, grimier man. The satchel contained a small, but beautifully ornate, statue of the great Pharaoh Ramses II and I was determined to get it back.

Several months of pain-staking work in the Valley of the Kings resulted in the discovery of the small statue, and it had been the most significant artifact found over the past year. A middle of the night raid by masked bandits resulted in the statue's disappearance, just days before the fruitful dig was to be toured by the Egyptian Director of Antiquities. Upon his visit, I vowed to get the statue back for his museum system and he agreed to provide all of his resources in that pursuit. A few of his leads led to this moment.

My peering continued in earnest and then my gaze wondered to the building directly across the street. Planning led to the selection of this spot, specifically due to the lower wooden frame of the neighboring buildings. I fell to one knee and loaded my crossbow with an arrow carrying a long, thin wire. Just as my targets were about to pass my position, I fired the crossbow at ankle height directly at the building across the way. The arrow silently cut through the air and slammed into the wooden frame. I quickly grabbed hold of the opposite end of the loose wire and pulled tightly. Immediately, passers-by began to trip over the almost invisible wire, my targets among them. The one carrying the satchel went head over heels, losing hold of the bag at the same time. As stunned bodies lay strewn in the street, I secured the satchel and blended into a near-by crowd. I was surprised to see the two men frantically pushing their way into the same crowd. Their heads swung in all directions attempting to catch a glimpse of the satchel. I removed the statue and placed it into my leather messenger bag, and then laid the satchel on a near-by barrel. Sliding back into the street, I headed directly to the Cairo Museum.

In short time, I reached the museum and carried the statue of the great pharaoh through the numerous and famous ancient Egyptian displays. By doing so, I felt a great sense of satisfaction; because I was reuniting it with many artifacts of the same nature and taking it to where it would be forever appreciated in history. I climbed the stairs to the suite of offices and walked into the wood-paneled reception room. The offices typically were a hectic environment and today were no different. I casually knocked on the large wooden door of the Director. He answered it himself, exchanged greetings, and quickly ushered me in.

'Professor Mane, so good to see you on this very hot day. What do I owe the pleasure?' He said as he leaned against the front of his desk.

'Business more than pleasure. I know that you're hoping that I'm here for a specific purpose, Director, and I won't disappoint you.' I replied standing before the bearded and well-dressed man.

'Ahhh…some of the leads have paid off I venture to guess?' He smiled widely.

'You could say that.' I answered while reaching into my leather bag. I handed him the statue, which was wrapped in a canvass material.

As he carefully unwrapped a part of his history, his eyes grew as wide as his smile. When the golden object appeared and glimmered against the light, I almost thought I heard a whimper.

'Stunning, isn't it?' I said. 'It was worth every effort to try to recover it in my book.'

'Yes…it certainly was. It certainly was, Professor.' He nodded continuously with the utterance of these words. 'Ramses the Great, was such a monumental figure in our history…I can almost feel his presence by holding this golden statuette. I can't wait to study this and display it in a place of significance here in the museum. It is awe inspiring… you never tire of finding such objects of historical significance. How can we ever thank you?'

'That's the business that I'm in, Director…finding history for the masses.' I laughed as I seated myself in a soft chair.

'Good at that you are too.' He said as he carefully placed the statue down on a table and then poured two drinks. 'Your reputation is well-known and respected…you also have a way of getting the job done no matter what the odds.'

'Vegas never scared me either.' I answered and took a sip of my drink through the heavy crystal.

'The daring are few and far between, Professor. There are items that the Department of Antiquities have wondered about for many, many years, but have made no real attempt to find. There are wonders out there in this great land…the treasures and artifacts that have yet to be found keeps one up at night.'

'You have many archaeologists at your disposal, why haven't you made the attempts?' I replied.

'Yes, but you need the right one. One who not only is good at his science, but also has the tenacity of a hound to search for his quarry.' The Director sat behind his desk. 'I know of many of the former, but few of the latter…such as you.'

'I'm guessing that there's a point to this conversation? Is there a specific object you had in mind?'

'Indeed....indeed!' He laughed. 'This is Egypt, where do I start? The greatest archaeological finds that this world will ever know are still out there, yet to be found. What it would mean to the museum to have some of them goes without saying.'

'If you had one to choose, Mr. Director, what would it be?' I smiled slyly with my drink in hand.

The Director's eyes bounced causally around the room filled with depictions of ancient Egypt. 'If I had to choose just one, then I would choose that which sits atop the bust of the pharaoh Tutmosis III.'

My eyes moved to the corner of the room where a gilded bust of the great pharaoh sat atop a marble pedestal. I paused and then turned to the Director. 'The Double-Crown of Egypt....'

He answered slowly. 'It would be the greatest single artifact of the century.'

'Possibly one of the greatest of all-time.' I answered. 'I'm not telling you anything that you don't already know, Director, but in all of the archaeological excavations in Egypt not one of the pharaoh's crowns has ever been discovered. Take into consideration the great number of pharaohs that ruled Egypt and...that fact is even more amazing.'

'Yes, that is so.' Replied the Director while scratching his chin. 'We've yet to completely come to a conclusion as why that is the case. We believe that the crowns were made of some form of material...a cloth of some nature...that deteriorated quickly, even in this arid climate.'

'Plausible conclusion,' I answered. But, I have another theory.'

'I'm interested to know, Professor. Please, what may that be?'

'There was only *one* Crown of Egypt and it was passed down from pharaoh to pharaoh through the centuries.'

'Hmmm…that is an interesting and wonderful theory.' He replied sitting forward in his chair. 'It would make it an even greater discovery.'

I also leaned forward. 'If my theory is correct, then the reason a Crown of Egypt does not sit here in the museum is that…*it* has never been found.'

'Wonderful,…a fantastic concept, Professor. May I commission you to test your theory then?'

'I'm in Egypt now…don't know when I would have an opportunity to return, so I'd be willing to test it while I'm here.'

'Let us toast to the adventure then.' Replied a smiling Director.

CHAPTER 2

Research

E GYPT HAS AN ABUNDANCE of hidden treasures, so many that it is difficult to know where to start. I have to admit, though, the pharaoh's crown would rank with the most valuable of relics and one that would garner a great deal of attention. I somehow seem to stumble into these adventures, but, hey…I think that's what I'm known for. Nothing happens on an empty stomach or with a parched palate…it was time to think over a plate of grub.

I strolled into my favorite place and asked for a seat towards the rear. It's easier to think when the lighting is low and large plants screen not only you, but somehow, your thoughts from escaping. The sweltering heat disappeared with my first drink, but as I removed the glass from my face, I saw a man standing before me. My quizzical look brought out a smile.

'Dr. Mane?' He asked with the smile.

'I've been called that…' I replied.

'I'm Dr. Meni…I met you in Pittsburgh several years ago. I'm also an archaeologist and was assisting the Carnegie Museum.'

A fleeting memory passed before me. 'You were working in the Egyptian exhibit…' I answered while completing the task of returning the glass to the table.

'Yes…Yes! You do recall.' He answered with glee. 'I recognized you from across the room as you entered.'

'Pleased to see you again, Doctor.' I offered my hand.

'Very much the same, Dr. Mane. It's an honor to have you here…and, may I ask, what brings you to Egypt?'

'I've been here for several months on a dig in the Valley of the Kings. Just completed my portion, but, as fate would have it, I've just been commissioned for another.'

'Your reputation precedes you, Doctor.' He said as he requested if he could have a seat and I obliged. 'You would be on your way home if it would not be something very worthy of your time.'

I smiled. 'Actually, it's getting to be winter in Pennsylvania…so I thought of sweating my butt off here a little longer. That's all.'

'I see…so what's the real story?' He replied with a prodding nod.

I looked him dead in the eye. 'From what I recall, Dr. Meni, you came with the highest of recommendations to the Carnegie, even so…I'm not sure if I'm entitled to release the information. Though, you may actually be able to tell me if it's even worth my time.'

'By all means….I will give you confidential privilege.' He answered with a proceeding wave of his hand.

I laughed. 'When items of high value are at stake, I'm not sure that just confidential privilege is going to do. You have to understand, this would be under the auspice of the Director of Antiquities. There would be a lot of red tape on my end if word would get on the street. I'm not even real fond of red.'

'Understood, Professor,' He smiled slightly. 'I have no wish to embroil you in government complications.'

I took another sip of my drink. 'I apologize for not being more frank, but…it is probably for the best at this point. May I keep you on retainer for reference purposes? Never know what you may find out that way.'

'Certainly, I'm very intrigued. Here's my card…I'm typically in Cairo, so I'm not hard to find.'

The following day was spent researching the subject of the Crown of Egypt. Even though I had just completed a dig, in my line of work, research is relaxation. The library was stifling and I wasn't certain if I would be better off in here or in some sand-swept portion of the Sahara. My knowledge of the crown's history was generally good, but I needed more detailed information if I were ever to find it. What I found was rather informing:

It's fairly-well a known fact that the primary crown of ancient Egypt, known as the Double-Crown, was a combination of the crowns of Lower and Upper Egypt. The history goes something like this:

King Narmer was an ancient Egyptian pharaoh of the Early Dynastic Period (c. 31st century BC). He is thought to be the successor to the pre-dynastic pharaohs Scorpion (or *Selk*) and/or Ka, and he is considered by some to be the unifier of Egypt and founder of the First Dynasty, and therefore the first pharaoh of unified Egypt. The identity of Narmer is the subject of ongoing debate, although mainstream consensus identifies Narmer with the First Dynasty pharaoh Menes. Menes is also credited with the unification of Egypt, as the first pharaoh. This conclusion is based on the Narmer Palette which shows Narmer as the unifier of Egypt and the two necropolis seals from Abydos that show him as the first king of the First Dynasty.

The White Crown of Upper Egypt (southern Egypt) was worn by King Narmer (often referred to as Menes) who was the first true ruler of ancient Egypt and considered to be the unifier. Depictions of the White Crown are visible as early as 3,000 BC. The Red Crown of Lower Egypt (northern Egypt) is depicted shortly thereafter and the Narmer Palette shows King Narmer wearing the White Crown on one side and the Red Crown on the other. Around the year 3,100 BC, the crown begins to be shown as the combined White and Red Crown (the Double Crown) and the lands of Upper and Lower Egypt are unified under one ruler.

White Crown

The White Crown of Upper Egypt (southern Egypt), formally known as the *Hedjet* in ancient Egypt, is a tall, conical headpiece, white in color and was worn as the primary crown of the Pharaoh. The White Crown is considered the first true crown of ancient Egypt. King Narmer, considered the first ruler of Egypt, wore the White Crown, which was deemed to be made of leather, cloth or felt stretched on a wire frame. This crown was depicted on the Narmer Palette as early as 3,000 BC and it is associated with the goddess Nekhbet.

Red Crown

The Red Crown of Lower Egypt (northern Egypt), formally known as the *Deshret* in ancient Egypt, was very distinctive in that it projected a curled wire from the top. The curled wire depicted the proboscis of a honey bee. The crown was possibly constructed of leather and cloth on a wire frame. The Red Crown was named after the land where its leaders ruled, the fertile Nile river basin. On either side of the Nile the desert land had a reddish hue and the name was derived from the color. The Red Crown is often associated with the goddess Neith.

The most intriguing of artifact yet to be discovered is the *Crown of Egypt*. The crown of Egypt was worn by every pharaoh from the Predynastic Period, through most of the dynasties in the ancient Egyptian era. The style and form changed through the centuries, but it was still the most consistent form of pharaoh attire used during the entirety of ancient Egypt.

The Double Crown of Ancient Egypt is a combination of the Red Crown and the White Crown. It is officially called the *Pschent,* but the Egyptians generally referred to it as *Sekhemti,* which translates as Two Powerful Ones.

This translation is fitting, since the White Crown represents Upper Egypt and the Red Crown Lower Egypt and together they are a symbolic representation of the pharaoh's power over both regions. The Double Crown also included the representation of a cobra (the uraeus) and a vulture, which were fastened to the front of the Pschent. The cobra represented the goddess Wadjet and the vulture the goddess Nekhbet, which is also why the cobra and the vulture were often referred to as the Two Ladies.

No Crown of Egypt – the Double Crown, has ever been found in archaeological excavations. Even in the most intact tombs ever discovered, such as that of the Pharaoh Tutankhamen, no traces of the elusive crown have been revealed. Generally, most of the crowns that the Pharaohs wore were made of either cloth, felt or leather and it is deemed that they were stretched over a wire frame. There were variety of shapes and styles, as well as colors and most were adorned with representative symbols with gold and possibly gems. Due to their construction, most of the crowns have never been discovered and are known to Egyptologists through wall depictions.

Crowns of ancient civilizations were primarily made of the strongest of materials, often with the most precious of metals and adorned with valuable jewels. These crowns could last centuries, but one made of cloth or leather, such as that of Egyptian Pharaoh's, could easily deteriorate in a much shorter period of time, if not appropriately preserved. The possibility does exist that there were a number of such Pharaoh's crowns and they didn't last the test of time. Though, I'm inclined to view this is a possibility, I'm also intrigued by the fact that not the slightest artifact remains of a possible crown. There would be possibilities that either the wire framing and/or leather fragments would have been found during an archaeological excavation.

I now fully realized the full extent of what this discovery could mean. Many Egyptian artifacts were made for each pharaoh, simply made distinct by the hieroglyphs and cartouche inscribed upon each. The pharaoh's royal crown appears to be the only one ever made and was ceremonially passed down from pharaoh to pharaoh. A one-of-a-kind, ancient and distinct artifact it certainly was. Its location is the secret of the millennium and my theories would have to be correct for any chance of it being discovered.

The question of where to begin is interesting. The Late-Period Pharaoh's ruled in northern or "lower" Egypt and where their burial grounds were located near Alexandria. The question is whether the Double-Crown was passed down to the Late Period and who would have worn it last?

This would have to be researched through hieroglyphic drawings depicting a certain pharaoh wearing the crown. I can be certain that the crown was worn from the Old Kingdom through a number of ancient Egyptian periods, namely, the First Intermediate Period, Middle Kingdom, Second Intermediate Period and the New Kingdom. These were the true Egyptian dynastic periods and the double crown would be worn during a majority of these periods. The research should commence with the subsequent periods when Egypt was ruled by foreign powers, such as in the Late Period, Ptolemaic and beyond. If the crown would disappear as an Egyptian symbol, this is when it would more than likely have occurred. This being the period between the last pharaoh of the New Kingdom, Ramses XI and the last Egyptian ruler, Cleopatra VII. Many of these foreign rulers attempted to maintain the Egyptian way of life and keep many of the dynastic traditions. This concept would help them govern the people of Egypt more easily.

I rented a vehicle and headed north towards Alexandria on the Egyptian Delta. The supplies I carried should last me a month, but I was already thinking of where to replenish the supplies as the need would have it. As a means of concealing the purpose of my search, the Director of Antiquities had implied that I was to work alone on this project. No one has ever searched directly for the crown before and if word hit the street that the search was on, it would attract interest from undesirable sources. The scarcity of the crown may make it the most valuable artifact in all of ancient Egypt.

CHAPTER 3

The Adventure Begins

I ARRIVED BY TRAIN IN Alexandria, the famed city named Alexander the Great, on the northern shores of Egypt. Here is where many of the post-dynastic rulers ruled Egypt. If the double-crown of Egypt was last used, it was here on the Mediterranean shores. I found a hotel room on the edge of the city and planned to travel back and forth from the dig sites. I immediately notified the Director of my intentions and whereabouts and requested some manual labor. The response came back quickly:

Dear Professor Mane,

We are operating under the utmost of secrecy in regards to this venture. If you believe that you have adequately secured a location of our quarry, I will provide security and labor at the site. Until then, I'm afraid you will be on your own. Careful as you tread. Thank You

Not exactly the response I was anticipating, but, then again, not surprising either. I can work without the local laborers to an extent, but if there is any heavy mound moving involved, I can see me collapsing on this thin mattress on a nightly basis.

I decided to start early in the next morning in order to investigate one of two sites I had designated, both of which were less than ten miles away. The Director did provide me with a Jeep, which I found on a side street near the hotel, the keys being handed to me by the hotel desk clerk on my way out. Weaving my way through the back streets and alleys of this ancient metropolis, avoiding a number of merchants and donkeys in the process, I soon found my way to open and dust covered roads.

This is the land of Cleopatra and the Late Period dynasties. The Tomb of Cleopatra has never been found and it would be ironic if I stumbled across the resting place of the famous queen – in an attempt to find an equally important ancient Egyptian artifact. As I travelled the long and dusty roads, the flat, dry lands called to me to find it's treasures… would I be able to answer?

I found my site that I had marked on my map and did an unusual and circular route to reach it so that the tire tracks could not be easily followed. It was always fun to have an excuse to drive in tight circles, make hair-pin turns and other maneuvers that covered my tracks. This location is one that I believed to be unexplored and may contain unknown tombs of Ptolemaic pharaohs…possibly the last who may have worn the Double-Crown. Many of these Late Dynasty tombs have been discovered and looted, but it is the best possible starting point at this juncture, in particular King Ptolemy IX, X and XI.

I unpacked the back of the Jeep, which was loaded with the equipment I would need to accomplish this one-man dig. Different shovels, trowels, hoes, sifters and various other pieces were moved to a small alcove by wheelbarrow. I walked the desolate location that already showed signs of looting before I even placed my shovel into the ground, but, this was to be expected. I noticed several pottery shards above ground and several deep holes, which made the looting very apparent. After a thorough walk around the tomb site, I took out my sketch pad and created a site survey and decided to begin very close to where my equipment was placed, which was an agreeable coincidence.

Looters rarely left much for history to find and the site showed certain signs of its impact. Several large holes and broken pottery shards made it clear that I was not the first to tread upon this parcel of dry ground. My best course of action was to begin excavation in the areas with the least disturbance, thus improving my chances of finding virgin ground.

I started with a stratification of the area and dug several test holes in four locations, only one of which appeared promising, which led me to dig several other test holes nearby. Hours of shoveling and excavating shortly left my arms tired and back tight. I made slight headway through what appeared to be an underground entrance with no evidence of previous excavation. Small slabs of limestone appeared approximately every foot and, after four such slabs appeared in succession, it was apparent that it was a stair case. I used the stairs to continue my dig downward, but I wished I had the help of additional manual labor.

After uncovering twelve stairs, I met a larger slab and discerned that I reached the bottom. This meant to begin a forward dig, as opposed to downward, for an entrance to obvious tomb laid before me. I determined that I would return the following day and continue my quest. In the meantime, I covered the newly found stairwell with two pieces of plywood I had brought with me for the purpose, which I then covered in sand. This was to keep any potential looters from spying the location from afar.

I don't recall the night, other than a quick meal and soon thereafter…a deep sleep. I awoke early, grabbed some strong coffee, loaded my satchel with the day's rations and headed off for the site before the great sun broke the horizon. I uncovered the stairwell and then studied my course of action, while sipping coffee and munching on a biscuit. Why couldn't there have been an Eat'n Park on my route like back in the 'Burgh?' I guess this crumbling, dry biscuit was going to have to do.

I descended the steps and immediately plunged a steel bar into the wall of sand before me. After several attempts, I hit a solid object some two feet deep. Pay dirt…literally. I shored up the surrounding area near the door to stave off a collapse of sand and then began to trowel my way through the packed sand that blocked the entrance. I uncovered a limestone slab the size of a door. I could really use some of the locals to help me move this massive stone, but the fact that it appeared undisturbed made it more important to keep this location a secret.

At the university, I had several discussions with professors in the engineering department for situations just as this. I asked them to provide advice on how to move such an object with limited man-power and equipment, which could not always be counted on in the field. I received several excellent suggestions and demonstrations on how to go about such a task and it appears that they would now pay off. I put to work pry bars, wedges and some elbow grease and, in an hour's time, I had moved the object enough to slide behind it.

I lit a lantern and turned on my flashlight. I had entered a vast area of tombs, most certainly of the Ptolemaic period, which is the dynasty when the Greeks ruled Egypt. They, though not truly Egyptian, were the last dynasty that attempted to keep the traditions of the ancient Egyptian pharaohs. They would have worn the famous double crown and the possibility existed that they would have been the last to do so. The crown could certainly have been left in the tomb of the last Ptolemy. The problem was I had no idea what Ptolemaic tomb I was in. Until I can find clear hieroglyphs, I will not know how far into history I have dug.

The hieroglyphs and drawings were certainly of the correct dynasty and the discovery of this tomb system was significant in its own right. With only the light from my lantern and flashlight to guide me, I found what I believed to be the main corridor and followed it. Yes, I passed many a tomb entrance along the path, but the tomb of the pharaoh would be deep in the tomb and certainly not easy to find. If I could find that primary tomb, I may find the crown of Egypt.

I walked cautiously, in particular since the light only covered some five feet in front of me and the air was stale and thick. I moved along a stone path and kept moving my eyes from the floor to the ceiling. You never knew what you could encounter in the tombs and traps were set to keep looters at bay.

Even with my deliberate scanning of the area, I tripped over a raised stone. I stopped in my tracks, but before I could move again, a taut rope flew out from between the stones and then, suddenly, one end snapped and the recoiling rope wrapped around my left leg. Immediately, the rope began to pull back in the direction of one of the tombs to my left.

I dove onto the rope to stop it, but the recoil strength was too powerful and the rope began to pull me towards the tomb. I laid the lantern on the ground to free my hands

I pulled my knife to try to cut the rope around my leg, but I couldn't reach it. It continued to drag me and I moved to my stomach to try to find something to grab hold of. There was nothing to be found, so I dug my fingers between two stones and grabbed hold with the tips of my fingers. The pulling stopped slightly, but I lost my grip and the rope jerked me hard and I was being pulled again.

I stood up trying to slow the movement and turned only to see the tomb door begin to open and the rope originating from inside. I was heading into a tomb and soon found myself pulled through the doorway. I slammed hard into a wall as the rope released. I quickly pulled my flashlight and reached for the machete. A sound from above led my flashlight in that direction and it revealed that the ceiling was moving downward. At the same time, the door was closing. I ran towards the door and it was already close to being closed. I jammed the machete between the frame and the door and it squealed as the movement slowed. I had enough room to slide out and I did so, pulling the machete with me at the last second. I'm no looter and I didn't deserve the fate.

Somewhat disheveled, I returned to my lantern and continued on towards the rear of the tomb complex. I saw some excellent drawings to my right and stopped to decipher them. They showed a pharaoh wearing the crown of Egypt. This was good news. Surprisingly, there were other depictions of pharaohs also and one of them was very distinctive…it was the Pharaoh Akhenaten. Akhenaten was a true Egyptian Pharaoh from a dynasty that ruled many years before the Ptolemy's. His depiction in this tomb was very interesting.

Next to this depiction were depictions of the latest line of Ptolemy's. This was not unusual for a site such as this, but the fact that it was near a depiction and cartouche of Akhenaten, really intrigued me. I moved my lantern throughout the vicinity looking for additional leads. The hieroglyphs were carved into the walls in this area, as opposed to painted, which was also somewhat unusual. Then, again to my amazement, carved depictions of a Ptolemy and one of Akhenaten sat side by side. On an altar near the two sat crowns, both were the double-crown of Egypt. How is that possible? Two crowns of Egypt...side-by-side...what does this imply? That the Ptolemy's had a crown, but there was another? Akhenaten's?

I ran the lantern and flashlight over the next line of hieroglyphs. The cartouche of Akhenaten appeared, again with the name of his capital – Akhenaten. Are they saying that Akhenaten's crown was different and that it still existed? I pulled out several pieces of parchment paper and made rubbings of the glyphs. This was a lead that could be worthy of following. I walked through the final areas of the tomb and quickly determined that there was nothing further to be found. Time to move the dig...to Amarna.

CHAPTER 4

An Unwanted Visitor

I RETURNED TO MY HOTEL, caught a quick nap and headed out for a bite to eat. Three days of exhaustive digging had my arms aching and my back tight, reaching for my wallet would be a notable chore. I sat outside of a large café, which had a pair of flimsy tents shielding its many patrons from the late afternoon sun as they enjoyed their supper.

It's ironic, but my next course of action was to follow the sun…actually, the Sun god, known in ancient Egypt as the Aten. I had a theory, a hypothesis, a hunch….whatever you want to call it and I planned to head to the once former capital of ancient Egypt, as brief as it may have been, called Amarna. I checked over maps of the area as the waiter brought my drink.

I casually sipped my drink and made notations on the map. The chatter of the other patrons was oblivious to me, but somehow I noticed a man walking towards my table. In my line of work, you keep your peripheral vision toned and your senses on a form of heightened alert.

He stood at my table before I bothered to lift my head. The face was very familiar.

'Professor Mane…now what do I owe the pleasure of your presence in Alexandria?' he said with a sly grin. My response was not immediate. 'If I know you,' he continued. 'It must be something I would be interested in also.' He chuckled while placing his cigarette back into his mouth.

'They still allow you out of your cage once in a while, do they, Marxum?' I answered while tipping my hat back.

'Always with the sharp wit you are, Professor. Of course, I'm still revered in the profession, regardless of your thoughts.' He replied while taking an uninvited seat at the table. 'Just taking a stroll…thought that you may enjoy some company for a few minutes.'

The middle-aged Russian was quite direct and dressed well, as usual. The brim of his small, nautical cap allowed the sun to peak to and from his face, creating a shiny beacon of his gold tooth.

'I know that some people do think highly of you,' I replied. 'But, you are aware that archaeology societies still find your tactics questionable.'

'We all have our methods, Professor...so to speak. I have a means to an end and I'm successful.' He took a drag on his cigarette.

'Did you light that cigarette with a stick of dynamite or do you just use it to blow up archaeological sites?'

'Come, come...Professor...you know that earth needs to be moved, at times, and I like to get there a little more quickly than others. That's all that it is.' He ordered a drink from the waiter.

I laughed. 'You are aware that the Director of Antiquities has you on the watch list, Marxum. One more bad move on your part and he'll have you deported.'

'I do have some slight inclinations regarding that point,' he answered gruffly. 'But,... my international reputation speaks for itself.'

I sat forward in my chair. 'He and the societies believe that you also intentionally "misplaced" the cache found at Siwa.'

'Again,' he replied with a wave of a hand. 'Pure speculation...maybe some jealousy...etcetera, etcetera. I've asked to participate in the investigation to find the artifacts...I have some excellent ideas.'

'I'm sure that you do.' I replied while folding my map.

'What have we here, Professor? A map of Amarna? Very interesting, I'm heading there myself very soon.'

'Should I ask…Why? Please come down after I've left, I'm in no mood to avoid dynamite blasts.'

'Work, of course. I'm just following up on a few leads I've developed over the years. I have a good staff now…made some recent hires and we'll see what they can do. Maybe we'll have the pleasure of meeting there? If so, the sun will shine upon us.' he smiled widely. 'Enjoy your meal, Professor…I shall take my drink and find an evening snack at the market.' He nodded and dropped a few coins on the table.

CHAPTER 5

Amarna

T HE DRIVE SOUTH TO Amarna was long and dry. This area is located north of Luxor and south of Cairo and on the east bank of the Nile River in the modern Egyptian province of Minya. I made several stops along the way at well-known ancient Egyptian sites in order to see a few colleagues who were working in the area and to gain some refreshment from the scorching sun. On my way south, I visited Giza, Saqqara, and Memphis on my impromptu archaeological tour.

Amarna, also referred to as el-Amarna or Tell el-Amarna is the capital city built by one of the most controversial pharaohs in Egyptian history, Akhenaten of the eighteenth dynasty. The city was called Akhenaten in ancient times, but currently, Amarna is an extensive Egyptian archaeological site that represents the remains of the city, which was only in existence for a twenty-year period.

The Pharaoh, who built this capital city, Akhenaten, was born Amenhotep IV to Amenhotep III and Queen Tiye. He is most well-known for being the first pharaoh to do away with the numerous Egyptian gods and direct the religious attention to one god, Aten, the Sun god. The pharaoh changed his name to Akhenaten, a tribute to his chosen deity and this earned him the title of "The Heretic Pharaoh." Akhenaten is credited with being the first leader in the history of the world to profess monotheism, which is the belief in only one god. This system of beliefs was not at all popular with the Egyptian public, who preferred the belief in numerous gods, also known as polytheism.

Akhenaten's wife was Queen Nefertiti, considered by most to be the most beautiful and important woman in all of Egypt. She is considered by many to have ruled as co-regent with her husband. Her famous bust, the Nefertiti Bust, is a staple of Egyptian artifact depictions. The bust is painted limestone and is believed to have been crafted by the sculptor Thutmose in 1345 BC. The Nefertiti Bust was discovered in 1912 by German archaeologist Ludwig Borchardt, who discovered it in Thutmose's workshop in Amarna, Egypt. The Bust has been in Germany since its discovery.

Akhenaten worshipped Aten, the disk of the sun, in ancient Egyptian mythology, and originally an aspect of Ra, who is considered as the creator, and giver of life. Furthermore, the god's name came to be written within a cartouche, along with the titles normally given to a Pharaoh, another break with ancient tradition. During the Amarna Period, the Aten was given a Royal Titulary (as he was considered to be king of all).

Akhenaten's son is believed to have been the most famous pharaoh in all of ancient Egypt, Tutankhamen or King Tut. The Pharaoh Tutankhamen, who was also known as the Boy King, was made famous primarily due to the fact that his tomb was discovered virtually intact, a very uncommon discovery. His greatest feat in life was to retract his father's beliefs in monotheism and returning Egypt to its polytheism system, primarily due to pressure from advisors. The worship of Aten was eventually said to have been eradicated by the Pharaoh Horemheb.

Upon arrival in Amarna, I secured a basic hotel room – if that's what you would call it – and drove directly to the location of the former capital, Akhenaten. This was not a desolate archaeological site and there were several other excavations on-going upon my arrival. I wasn't familiar with any of the supposed three other teams involved in the Amarna area digs and, based upon the Director's request, I planned to keep a low profile while I was here. This is not to say that I wouldn't have a brief conversation with the other teams, because their insight could save me days of work. I just couldn't reveal what I was looking for…specifically.

I had an idea of where I wanted to begin my dig, which would be in the area of the royal palace. I was informed that none of the other teams were working in that section, which was certainly a bonus, but I wanted to make sure and walked in that direction. I viewed only one of the teams on my trek; they were busy uncovering the remains of a market just east of my destination.

After a thorough field survey, I could certainly see the semblances of a settlement pattern and I derived what was once the former palace's gate. I pulled out my drawing of the palace and moved towards the main entrance for this is where I would begin my excavation. There was little still existing of what was once a grand building and what did exist would be buried beneath the sand. I sketched a few depictions on my map, added a few notes and walked back to the Jeep. I would create a plan for the excavation and then return for a better view of the area from atop a near-by hillside later this evening….too hot to go there at present.

I drove back to town and looked for possible places to eat and relax. There were a couple of possibilities in this small locale. I went back to the room and freshened up, before heading for a shady spot near the hotel for some much needed rest. Soon, evening set in and I awoke refreshed. I grabbed a sandwich from a street vendor and made my way to the Jeep for a return to the site, specifically, a near-by hillside so that I could view the whole area.

I slowly climbed the gradual hill while viewing the entire City of Akhenaten on my evening ascent. The sun was setting over the horizon, but its' piercing rays still cracked the Egyptian sand. The slight breeze increased the higher that I climbed and to a point where it actually became refreshing just as I reached the top. It was apparent that the other archaeological teams were taking advantage of the cooler temperatures and several workers could be seen still toiling at this hour. Through my binoculars, I could see that each dig was represented in the three specified locations.

I could also see the area where I planned to begin, basically at the palace gates, but I couldn't make out much detail even with the binoculars. I scanned the areas near the palace and looked for possible entry points from this vantage point. A couple of possibilities became noticeable, which didn't appear as having potential from ground level. I sat down on a large rock and made some notations on the site plan as the slight breeze ruffled my papers. I continued viewing the former capital city and adding to my map with detail that was not present.

Before I left and before the sun hid behind the horizon, I went back to my binoculars to scan the entire area once more. I pinpointed the area where I planned to start my dig and then scanned the locale of the other teams...one...at the market dig...two...just east of them...three...at the southern perimeter of the city...four...in the far north. Four? There was supposed to be only three? I had just looked over the entire area a half-hour before and only noticed three...my notes even state that I viewed three teams.

I focused the binoculars on the fourth team in the far north. I could see at least three individuals moving about, but they were partially hidden behind a small knoll. This team was also the furthest from my current location and their activities were the least discernable. I'm interested to know about this team, since the documents from the Director stated that only three were here - and their approximate locations - and this was not one of the locations notated. I made a point to take a closer look tomorrow and then began my descent back to the Jeep. I returned to the village, which now was filled with the locals on their evening stroll, and sent a message to the Director asking about the group working in the north.

CHAPTER 6

Search for the Palace

T HE NEXT MORNING I awoke early and spent the first half-hour loading the Jeep with supplies and equipment. Here in Egypt, you have to start early when the weather is cool or get to an underground location by the late-morning sun. Of course, as I viewed yesterday, the evening is also a possibility for above-ground work.

I sped off from the small hotel, rousing nothing but chickens as I made my way out of town. I raced against the rising sun that began to peak in the distance and made my way to the site before it was totally over the horizon. I drove the Jeep right up to the dig location and backed it against an ancient wall that protruded from the sands. I propped a small tent against it for shade and this would be my above-ground base of operations. Once again, I cursed the fact that I could not have assistance on this dig, but I had little time to think about it. I laid the map out on a table set-up under the tent and determined where I thought it best to begin. After a very intensive stratigraphy of the area, I performed some sampling, which really confirmed that I was in the right location. Shards of broken pottery were found in one sample and two of the pieces depicted Aten, the sun god.

My theory was that the palace maintained two sets of stairs upon entrance. One rose to the main foyer of the palace and the other staircase descended. The second staircase was my quarry, since whatever I was to find here was deep in the sand. A massive sub-basement was what I believed to exist below the main floor. My shovel hit the ground and hours of toil and labor would soon follow…again, I cursed the fact that a couple of extra set of hands could not be had.

Time moved slowly and the heat increased rapidly, but I was making headway. I had uncovered what appeared to be a pathway that led to the palace doors. Block after block of limestone appeared under several feet of sand on a path approximately ten feet wide. A small wall appeared on each side and it was adorned with hieroglyphs of the god Aten at specified intervals. In many cases, the discovery of this path would be worthy of front-page material in every newspaper in the western world, but, for me, it was only the beginning.

Soon, just as I had experienced in Alexandria, the semblances of a descending stairwell appeared, but much greater in size. This was a palace stairwell that once matched an identical ascending staircase that led to the main palace floor. Unfortunately, the sands of time left little of the latter, other than what may have been the base of the primary floor. The main floor has had various degrees of excavation, but no one has ventured to the sub-floor, mostly due to not receiving permission from the Director of Antiquities...until now.

I uncovered five steps through great effort, but I did not venture to uncover their entire length, which I would guess to be fifteen feet wide. I would leave a full excavation to a later archaeological crew, since my primary goal was to clear a four-foot path right down the center of the stairwell, which would be sufficient to satisfy my needs. I shored up the sand walls from collapsing and covered the site. My work for today was done and just before the heat of the day would make its presence known.

I had no plan to leave for the day, at least not before briefly speaking with the other crews in the area and, in particular, checking out the unknown fourth group in the northern part of the city. It was a common courtesy to make contact with crews nearby, primarily so that they will know that you are in the area and that you're not here on an illegal dig looking for artifacts to sell on the black market.

I made my rounds and had interesting discussions with the other crews, who were Egyptian and British. They provided some information that would assist me, in particular, on geological aspects. I wasn't familiar with anyone that I met, but I did recognize one archaeologist's name from a book on excavations in the Valley of the Kings, which I had read a couple of years ago. The most interesting part of my discussions with the teams was they were not aware of the fourth team in the northern sector...they thought I was to be the fourth team in the Amarna area.

I immediately headed in the direction where I noticed the fourth group working. It was a decent walk, but I chose to do so, as opposed to driving up in the Jeep and attracting attention. When I neared the area, I climbed the remains of a building to get a better view. Keeping myself from being seen, through my binoculars, I could see what appeared to be fairly large operation at work. There were two large tents and a few smaller ones, as well as three vehicles. A number of local workers could be seen scurrying around moving and sifting sand and there were several people in the tents. Whatever was going on was not being done by a fly-by-night outfit, but they may have chosen this location since it can only be seen from a higher vantage point.

I climbed down from my perch and began to weave my way through the remains of various structures with the intention of getting a better view. I moved to within 25 yards of the work site, but still couldn't discern the intention of the dig. They were definitely working on a certain area, but my view was impeded. A crew of six local workers could be seen at the current time and what appeared to be an archaeologist standing with his back to me. Inside one of the larger tents I could see several more people who were either seated or walking about.

After a short time, a person emerged from the tent, a Caucasian dressed in kakis, who walked up to the other archaeologist who had his back to me. They exchanged a few words and kept their eyes on the work begin done before them, all the while, jotting a few notes in their respective tablets. They both wore hats, but one of them definitely looked familiar. I pulled out my binoculars and focused in on the two men who had their backs towards me.

I held my gaze until I could get at least a profile view of the pair. Finally, the first one walked a short distance away to look at something and I could see his face....not familiar. With his back still to me, the other continued to jot notes, but the thin, slight frame and small head definitely looked familiar. Suddenly, he turned and walked in the direction of the other and his face came into view. No! It couldn't be…. Waterhouse! How did that weasel end up here?

I instinctively slouched down even more, now that I believed that I could be more easily recognized. After a minute, I realized who I was hiding from and returned to my original position. Waterhouse is someone who may struggle finding the pencil in his pocket, let alone spot me peering through a few cracks. I continued my surveillance of the site and I could see him walking around in a perceived authoritative manner. He made gestures and pointed to specific areas at the site, all in his demeanor of attempting to prove his worth.

I have to admit that Waterhouse, my former student, was a bookworm and knew the subject of archaeology well…after all, I taught him. But, he had very little practical ability of moving that knowledge to actual field work. Though, try telling him that…he's a legend in his own mind. I last spoke to him six-months ago in Italy. He was still basking in the glory of finding what people have called the *Stone of the Sahara*. He tripped over the stone when he was last in Egypt, but, nevertheless, he did find it.

He tried to parlay the notoriety into fame and women, neither of which would ever come easily with his 130-pound frame and cartoon character looks. He's the type of guy who would be bragging about a great adventure of his in the desert and then pass out at the site of a spider walking past his shoe. I last heard from him via his Christmas card where he told me of his many accolades after finding the stone and that he didn't have time to get in touch, due to jet-setting around the world on speaking engagements…he had slipped away to send me the card. I didn't have the heart to tell him in my reply that I noticed the Peoria, Illinois postmark…his hometown.

Nevertheless, he was here and I needed to know how he came onto this team that was not known to the Director, as of my last contact. I waited until he was alone towards the far edge of the site and tossed a stone in his direction. As the stone landed near him, he first looked to the sky and then, sensing danger as only he would, he apparently became wary and hid behind a partial wall. I now had him where I wanted him, which was out of direct site.

I snuck up on him from behind and grabbed him around the midsection, while covering his mouth. The latter move was to prevent a girl-like scream from echoing through the valley. He struggled and flailed wildly – like a girl – and I could hear his muffled voice saying that he knew karate, as he threw a few "chops" in the air in a scare tactic. Of course, he didn't know karate and my laughter was even more startling to him.

I finally swung him around where he could see me and his eyes literally "bugged" out of his head. I held a finger to my lips in a quieting gesture and slowly released my hand from his mouth.

'Professor!' he blurted as he sank to the ground with one hand still poised for a deadly karate chop.

'Calm down and be quiet, Waterhouse…yes, it's me.' I said while I offered a hand to lift him to his feet.

'Wha…what are you doing here?' he rose slowly. 'Wow, you shouldn't sneak up on me like that, Professor…I may have hurt you.' He confidently brushed himself off.

'I'll keep that in mind.' I replied with a slight chuckle. 'I don't want to be seen, so let's keep it down, okay?'

'Sure…sure, Professor. What's going on? Why are you here?' His eyes were still bulging from his head and his body still hadn't stopped shivering.

'I'm working at this site, just about a half-mile from here.' I replied. 'Who are you working with and when did you show up?'

45

'We just got here a day or so ago…I'm working for him.' He pointed to someone just exiting the tent nearby. We couldn't be seen from where we stood, so I was able to peer closely.

'Marxum! You're working for Marxum!' I answered in an aggravated, but hushed tone.

'You know him? Mr. Marxum was looking for some highly qualified archaeologists and, of course, sought me out.' He smiled smartly and pulled his pants up. 'You know…the whole Stone of the Sahara thing… I'm now in demand.'

'Yes, he deserves you.' I replied while rolling my eyes.

'Are you here to recruit me too, Professor?' He shook his head. 'I don't know, but I can see what I can do…fit you in somehow…you know, since I'm already on the site.' He removed his pith hat and brushed back his hair. 'I may be able to, at least, provide some consultation on your dig, etc. Anything for you, of course.'

I looked around the partial wall towards the tents. Marxum was now discussing something with those moving sand. 'I think I'll be fine… you're too busy, Teddy. This whole dig here may collapse if I pull you away. What's the purpose of this team being here anyway?'

'According to Mr. Marxum, he believes that there is a tunnel here that leads directly to Akhenaten's palace. They would use it bring people to and from the palace without being seen. He's sees great potential in the site.'

'Marxum is looking for a tunnel, huh? Don't let me see you light a dynamite fuse, Waterhouse…I'll have all of your licenses pulled myself. By the way, don't tell him that I'm here…yet.'

'Dynamite? Haven't seen any, but, they haven't granted me access to everything right now.'

'Keep your eyes open.' I answered. 'Are you staying in the village?'

'The team has a camp just outside the village…nice set-up actually.'

'OK, make your way into town tonight around seven and I'll meet you at the hotel. We'll talk later.' I shook his hand and quietly slipped away. Waterhouse returned to the site and I could hear him say something concerning the locals going about their work "all wrong" and that he would be giving a professional demonstration on how to do it "correctly" in about an hour.

CHAPTER 7

Waterhouse

T HE SUN WAS STILL rather high as seven o'clock rolled around. I went downstairs and decided to wait in the small lobby for Waterhouse to show. No one else was present, outside of the desk clerk who was busy sorting keys. There were a few chairs and I sat down in one where I could see the street. The area was still bustling at this hour with people taking advantage of the cooler temperature. Vendors shopped their wares on blankets across the street, as several food carts made their way up the road.

After ten minutes of mindless relaxation, I noticed the smallish, gawky frame of Teddy Waterhouse weaving his wave through the crowd. He tipped his hat to several people and tipped it even lower to the women. Of course, no one paid attention, but it appears that it made him feel important.

A few minutes later, I met him at the hotel door. 'Hungry?' I asked.

'Famished...' He replied panting from his walk. 'You know me, Professor...I eat like a horse to stay in top condition in this environment.' Waterhouse weighed a good 130 pounds dripping wet.

I waved to a passing food cart, which quickly moved in our direction. We each chose a food item for our evening meal and headed inside for my room. We sat around a small table and I broke out a few beverages that I had been keeping cold.

'Tell me, Professor, what your dig entails?' he asked with a mouthful. 'I mean, you didn't mention it in your Christmas card.'

'I'm working for the Director of Antiquities on a project. Sorry, Waterhouse, I can't let you in on the purpose at the moment.' I said as I swallowed.

'Director of Antiquities....!' He said somewhat loudly. 'You're working on a top-secret, government project!? Oh, man! You're going to need me...'

'I'll manage for now. I'm more interested in *your* dig.'

'Fair is fair, Professor…I know that you can't reveal much with it being a top-secret government project and all, but you can tell me what you're looking for. That's all…I won't ask for details. Heck, I won't even ask where you're digging.' He smartly broke a piece of bread and stuck it in his mouth.

I stared at him. 'Let me think about it. As for your dig, do you know if it's been authorized by the Director's office?'

'You know, I'm so busy when working on these high-level projects that I don't have time to look for small details like that, but it's a coincidence that you ask.' He sat forward in his chair. 'Just after you left today, a Jeep rolls up and this smartly, dressed Egyptian guy gets out and asks for Mr. Marxum. He's carrying a brief case and opens it in the tent and hands Mr. Marxum a piece of paper. I asked Fallory, the other archaeologist, what it was all about and he said that we were finally authorized for the dig. So, I guess it's full-tilt now.'

'Okay, so you believe that's the case and I can double-check that, of course.' I answered taking a swig of my drink. 'Actually, I spoke with Marxum a while back in Alexandria and he did mention that he was coming here.'

'That's all I know, Professor. So, if I might ask, what does the government have you working on…I'm intrigued?' He had a wide smile on his face and his leg jittered with excitement.

'I can't tell you. I don't think the Director would appreciate it if I release that information.'

'Now, come on. I gave you some information and you know that I'm one of your trusted colleagues out here in this vast desert. People like us need to stick together…never know when you'll need my skills to bail you out. I mean…assist in any way that I can.' He chewed nervously as he viewed my stoic expression.

'Sorry, Waterhouse…maybe in time.' I replied while continuing with my meal.

'So, that's it…You know, as your former student, I'm still trying to learn…on-the-job. But, I guess that the teaching ends in the classroom… that's what I hear.' He leaned back in his chair and wiped his mouth. 'That's fine…I understand.'

'Okay…Okay…' I held up my hands. 'Look…If I tell you it's in the strictest of confidence. You may be right…since I'm working alone, I may need someone that I can somewhat trust to give me a hand in a certain situation and you happen to be…*unfortunately*…the only one near-by.'

'Anytime…anytime, Professor. I'm always looking for adventure.' He tucked his napkin into his shirt confidently.

I told him of my search for the Crown of Egypt, which made his mouth drop open and his eyes bulge once again. I swore him to secrecy, we finished our meal and I sent him back to camp before anyone became uneasy about his absence.

The following days were filled with heavy excavation on my part, as I made my way further down the stairwell. I ran into several obstacles from an apparent cave-in many centuries past and this severely delayed my approach to the bottom, much to my chagrin. With the massive amount of work, sore back, and blistered hands, a fleeting thought would even pass to ask Waterhouse for an occasional hand. Then again, I might have gotten only an hour or so of work out of him before his frail frame would collapse in exhaustion.

On the third day of such exhaustive work, I heard my name being called from the entrance of the stairwell and it was obviously that of

Waterhouse. I slowly climbed my way towards the top and met him in the middle.

'Professor! Professor!' He repeated on his way down. 'I need to talk to you.'

'What's going on Waterhouse? Did you drive here or walk all the way?'

'I walked…I didn't want to have them see me come here, so I told them I was going for a walk on my lunch break.'

'Okay, what's so important that you made that long trek?'

'He knows! He knows about your dig.' He answered out of breath.

'Who knows? Marxum?' I replied holding him by the shoulders.

"Yes! Yes…Mr. Marxum and boy did his eyes light up!'

I sighed and leaned against the wall. 'Well, everyone would have found out sooner or later, but I was hoping to get a month or so in before it would be revealed. If so, I could have had some labor assistance and security at the site by then. How did he figure it out?'

'Well, I sort of told him…' Waterhouse replied stammering.

I grabbed him by the shoulders again and looked him sternly in the eye. 'You told Marxum what I was looking for!?'

'Well…I sort of had too.' He was shaking and stumbling over his words.

'I swore you to secrecy, Waterhouse! Of all people…Marxum! Why would you have 'had' too…Teddy….Why?'

'Well…you see… it was like this….' He shook his head as spoke. 'I was looking over a few maps…they were key maps of the dig… and I saw something interesting and brought it the attention of Marxum and Fallory. We were looking over the map spread out on the table and I sort of spilled my.....coffee...all over it.' He continued the head shaking. 'Plain out obliterated the map...bad ink and all.'

'And......' I urged him to continue.

'And...he was furious, since it was the only map of that section...a key section...that he had. He said that it could set the dig back for a month or more or even end it.'

'So, what does this have to do with you telling him what I was searching for?'

'He threatened to fire me and I begged him not too, but he seemed like he had his mind set.'

'He was going to fire you over spilling coffee on a map?' I asked.

'Well, it wasn't my first mishap...you know.' He answered quietly.

'You're kidding...You? Have mishaps? Don't even tell me, Waterhouse...I don't want to know.'

'It's all good, Professor...nothing really major...'

'I don't want to know.' I replied and looked away.

'Truck will be fine...' He insisted on continuing.

I held up my hand, but he continued.

'Once we find the wheel.....couldn't have gone far...except for over the cliff...what are the odds of that...you know?'

I held my hand to my head. 'So...tell me why you told him...'

'He threatened to fire me, but then said we could make a deal. He said that he knew you were here – you told him so in Alexandria – and he wanted to know why? He said that he was aware that I was a former student and had worked with you...once.'

'And you told him.' I replied still in the same position.

'I had too...my entire reputation as a top-notch archaeologist would have been ruined if I had been fired. I didn't see any real harm in it. He can't take over your dig or anything with the government's involvement...I'm real sorry, Professor...I really am, but I sort of had to tell him.' He dropped his head.

'Okay...Okay...you told him, Waterhouse. He knows. Just keep him busy at that dig and out of my hair. If you hear anything related to this site...you come to me real quick and tell me...got it?'

'Yes...Yes...of course, Professor. You can count on me...I owe you one now.' He actually broke a slight smile. "I have to get back...I'll talk to you soon.' He hurried back up the stairs and was soon out of sight.

CHAPTER 8

The Doctor Arrives

D URING THE FOLLOWING DAYS, I made head-way in my excavation and finally reached the bottom of the stairwell or, at least, a section of it. The doorway that I found was stacked with large stones and my next move would be to move them to ground level. That is a task that would be difficult for one person.

I also received a reply from the Director, who confirmed that Marxum's dig was authorized, but with reservations. Knowing his reputation, this was understandable. The Director also informed me that he was finally authorizing some assistance on my site, but it would be an Egyptian archaeologist. He phrased it to say that it would be someone I would find "acceptable." He also stated that he should be able to join me the day after the telegram was received.

While moving stones with a pry bar the following day, I heard a call from above and climbed the stairs to investigate. The outline of man stood at the top of the stairwell, shadowed against the bright sun. To my surprise it was Dr. Meni, the archaeologist that I had met in Pittsburgh and, again, just recently in a restaurant in Cairo. He stated that he had had a meeting with the Director the week before and mentioned that he had spoken to me recently. The Director, knowing of our previous acquaintance and of my need of assistance, asked him if he'd be interested in joining in the search. After he was apprised of the purpose and progress, he obliged.

Dr. Meni wasted no time in grabbing another pry bar and assisting in the stone removal. With his assistance, we were able to create a small hole in the doorway, just large enough for someone to crawl through. As we worked, I filled Dr. Meni in on what I had accomplished and found. In return, he gave me some important insight into the crown's history and whether or not he felt this endeavor worthy. He also revealed that the Director wanted him here to assist in keeping an eye on Marxum.

Later that evening, we sat at an outdoor café enjoying a beverage. 'So, tell me Doctor,' I started as I refilled our glasses. 'Do you agree with my theory of finding the crown here in Amarna?'

'Yes, Doctor, I do.' The well-dressed Egyptian replied. 'Might I add that you may find a crown...*a* double-crown of Egypt.'

I swirled my glass. 'But not the *official* double-crown...?'

'That would be my theory, Dr. Mane. This is certainly a logical location to excavate with it being a former capital and the fact that the lower-level of the palace has never really been excavated.' He took a brief drink. 'The entire lower-level wasn't really known until you found them in your research. Somehow, you just beat Marxum to the discovery. If he finds the tunnel he is in search of he will most likely discover that it leads to a lower-level.'

'I think that he may already know.' I replied shaking my head. I proceeded to tell him of Waterhouse revealing the purpose of my search. 'I can assure you that Marxum visited my site when I left for the day...at some point. If so, he will have noticed that I had uncovered a stairwell.'

'Well then, Doctor,' Dr. Meni replied while sitting straight up in his chair. 'That is unfortunate, since the race is now on, so to speak.'

'How so?' I answered matching his movement.

'You have found a stairwell...Marxum has discovered a tunnel...both of which lead to the lower-level of the palace. He now knows of the possible existence of the crown in that lower-level and I assure you that he will stop at nothing to find it *first*.' He shook his head.

'The thought has crossed my mind.' I answered while looking to the sky, which was just now beginning to reveal its twinkling stars. 'I've also thought of ways to slow him down.'

'Such as?' Dr. Meni asked.

'I can send word to the Director of this possibility and request that his excavation be slowed with some form of government red-tape. I know I can make that happen…maybe even have him send some observers to his dig. I also have another plan, but I'm not even sure I want it to happen.' I took a long drink.

'What might that be, Doctor? Let's not rule anything out yet.'

'Stealing Waterhouse from him and allow him to work with us.' I sighed and rolled my eyes. 'I know, I know…I explained what a pain he can be, but, I must admit…he's on that dig because he's the most technically sound person they have. Taking him away would hamper Marxum and, if he assists us, that would give us a hand.'

'Something to consider.' Meni replied. 'He's not under contract with Marxum, he can leave at any point.'

I nodded. 'I'll have a talk with him tomorrow.'

CHAPTER 9

Marxum

AFTER A FULL DAY where Dr. Meni and I only studied maps, I was able to have Waterhouse meet us at the hotel the following evening, and I brought up the subject of having him join Dr. Meni and me on our expedition. He, of course, made statements to the effect that he knew it would only be a matter of time that I would ask and that he had a difficult decision to make, since he was the most sought after archaeologist in all of the Middle East. I clearly informed him that I was doing him a favor and that he was one broken pencil away from being fired by Marxum…and his reputation would go with it.

He strutted around the room confidently, lamenting on the whether anyone could imagine his dilemma of being such a "wanted man" and how upset that Marxum would be at the loss of his expertise. I snapped a pencil that I was holding and he quickly sat down saying that he would quietly slip out of Marxum's camp the following day.

At the site the next day, Doctor Meni and I made significant progress in shoring up the stairwell and doorway to avoid a potential collapse. We decided not to remove much of the rubble in the doorway, since it appeared to be bracing a cracked wall. With a large enough of an entrance for us to slide through, there was no real necessity to make the entrance larger. Later in the day, we shined a torch through the opening, but couldn't see much. After accumulating our gear, we slid through the opening in the doorway to get our first view of what existed on the other side.

Flashlights and a torch hit the darkness like a Broadway stage. To our pleasure, there were no obstructions nearby and we could see a corridor disappearing into the blackness. The air was a little thick and dusty, so we covered our nose and mouth with handkerchiefs for filtering purposes. We walked through the sand-covered corridor, which showed an occasional movement of a scurrying reptile. Snakes were a big concern and we used a tactic of swinging a walking stick several feet in front of us, point in the sand, as a means of scaring off anything in our path. Doctor Meni had attached his flashlight to his swinging stick, so that anything in the sand could be seen.

Surprisingly, we encountered no additional blockages for the next three-hundred feet. The tunnel we were apparently following became more elaborately decorated and wider every ten to twenty feet. As we slowly continued our trek, we could hear slight rumblings coming from ahead of us, but still significantly in the distance. The rumblings were spaced every five minutes and they caused dust to pour from above our heads.

'What might that be, Doctor?' Dr. Meni asked. 'They are not natural sounds.'

'It's dynamite.' I replied reluctantly. 'Marxum is at it again…he's blasting his way through some debris on the far end of this tunnel.'

'Dynamite!' Dr. Meni exclaimed. 'How dare he use that in an archaeological site again?!'

'He doesn't care, Doctor. He wants to reach his goal as quickly as possible. He has no concern of what lays in his path along the way… only his prize…in this case, literally at the end of the tunnel.'

'And Waterhouse…where might he stand with all this?'

'My guess is that he already slipped out and is on his way here.'

A voice burst out from behind us, several hundred feet away. 'How right you are, Professor Mane….how right you are. Sound travels well down here, doesn't it?' Based on the accent, the voice was certainly that of Marxum.

Dr. Meni and I turned quickly and could see several flashlights and two torches working the darkness. 'Stay where you are, Professor…we're here to escort you back to the surface. You're dig is effectively closed.'

'What are you talking about Marxum and why the hell are you using dynamite again after you've been warned time and time again?!' I answered angrily.

'Enough, Professor! Your man Waterhouse left our dig right while we were preparing to move deep into this tunnel. We were wondering where he was going...so, we followed. He came right here amazingly. We just had to see what the great Professor has discovered and here we are. Now, come with us quietly – you've now infringed upon the area that I'm authorized to excavate.' The voice became louder and the numerous flashlights brighter as they neared. 'I must warn you...we are armed.'

I motioned to Dr. Meni to drop to his knees and to stay quiet. I quickly pulled out my miniature cross bow from my bag. 'That'll be the day, Marxum!' I fired off three quick arrows towards the flashlights and they split the cold, stale air with force. I could only imagine their horror of the sound of a streaming object approaching them.

We heard a couple of "thuds" and voices in sheer shock and pain, which made it clear that my targets had been hit. 'Stay where you are, Marxum, or I'll hunt all of you down.'

'Let's turn off our flashlights, Doctor.' I said quietly to Dr. Meni. I took the torch and planted it in the ground and we moved behind its light. "We'll have the advantage in the darkness.'

'There are a number of us down here, Professor Mane...do you have that many arrows?' Marxum shouted loudly. We could hear voices stating that they were taking the injured to the surface. We then heard another scream and we could see the flashlights hitting the ground searching for something.

'Better watch those snakes too, Marxum...this is a dangerous place.' I answered and then we moved to the far wall so that they could not track my voice. Suddenly, a canister was thrown in our direction and we could hear the release of some form of gas. I motioned to Dr. Meni to cover his nose and mouth and instructed him to follow me. We followed the wall and headed directly towards Marxum and his men, who had fallen back to avoid the gas. They moved quickly in reverse, never noticing that we were right behind them and not still deep in the tunnel.

I actually caught up to one of the men and slammed him head-first into the wall. We continued to follow the wall in the darkness towards the exit, but were thirty yards behind the group jogging in the same direction. At one point, I felt an opening in the wall and stopped to wait for Dr. Meni. I fired a quick flashlight beam into the opening and saw it was a doorway. I pulled the Doctor towards me and the two of us laid a shoulder into the door, which burst open. We closed the wooden door behind us and immediately turned on the flashlights. We felt safe for Marxum and his gang would not venture back down the tunnel for some time, fearing the lingering effects of whatever gas was contained in those canisters. We sealed the bottom of the door with sand to keep any remnants of it from leaking into our location.

The flashlights barely dented the darkness and little could be seen. The air was thick and heavy. Centuries had passed since the last ancient Egyptian crossed the threshold into this room. 'We need a torch, Doctor…let's see if we can find something to light.' I said as I slowly slipped into the darkness.

After a brief search that led to some debris to my right, I found some flammable material that could be tied to a stick. I met Dr. Meni at our original location and lit the improvised torch. The area brightened quickly, almost as though it had been starved of light. Several statues of ancient Egyptian gods stood before us, flanking a hallway some 50 feet ahead.

'This is amazing, Doctor Mane!' Dr. Meni exclaimed with wide-eyes. 'Ancient Egyptian gods in Akhenaten's palace!'

'Yes, he was the first and only pharaoh to believe in one god - monotheism, but there's Hathor, Ptah and Isis…really odd. I'm starting to believe that this is where he stored the statues…keeping them out of public site. Even he was afraid to destroy them.' I spoke as we moved closer to the figures.

'Look, Doctor,' I said pointing to the hallway ahead. 'There are numerous hieroglyphs on the walls. They should give us an idea of where we are.'

Using the torch and flashlights, we both scanned the hieroglyphs, which lined the walls on both sides from top to bottom. 'Right here, Doctor,' I said pointing half-way up the left wall. 'It states…generally… Akhenaten, per the cartouche…royal chamber…dynastic treasures… protected by the gods…as their only duty. Temple of Aten!'

'Yes, Doctor Mane, it's saying that the gods only have one remaining duty in ancient Egypt…to protect the treasures of the dynasty and the Temple of Aten – the Sun god. That is why the statues are in front and I'm sure that we'll find more.'

'Well,' I replied pointing my flashlight into the vast darkness ahead of us. 'It's referring to dynastic treasures and temples. We could be in a repository of some sort. Can we have been so fortunate that Marxum actually led us to what we were looking for?'

'I don't think that there is a better location for the crown, if it's here.' Dr. Meni replied while wiping his forehead with a handkerchief. 'The crown is one of the greatest treasures of any dynasty.'

CHAPTER 10

Peril in the Palace

T HE DOOR AT THE end of the baroque corridor, though it squealed with centuries of non-use, opened much easier than ever anticipated. A rush of surprisingly colder air hit us as the door opened wider. After ensuring that it would reopen, we closed the door and braced it from the inside with a metal rod that appears to have been used for the purpose.

The torch light led us to another wide and ornate corridor with numerous doorways on either side. We assumed that each room held a treasure of the dynasty during the palace's heyday. We took a methodical approach and entered the rooms on the right in order. The first several were empty, but showed the remnants of shelves and tables carved into the granite. This is where the dynastic treasures were displayed. The fourth room on the right included a stairway. I told Dr. Meni to stay in the room and I would ascend the steps and see what awaited us above.

I carefully climbed the steps, checking each step before placing my foot, and made it past the first five. I motioned to Dr. Meni that I was continuing when the sixth step slightly sank below my weight.

'The step moved...' I said while bracing myself on the walls.

'It may be just loose...put your light on it and make sure.' Dr. Meni answered.

I swung the flashlight downward and could see that the steps were not independently carved, thus creating thoughts that I may have stepped into something...literally.

'I hear a rumble from below the staircase!' I said as the vibrations increased.

'I can hear them too...try to come back down.' Dr. Meni implored.

Just as I turned, the step gave way, as did all of the steps below me that were visible. I gained my balance and stood on a few pieces of the steps that did not collapse, but there was no possibility of going back down the stairwell.

'Are you alright??' Dr. Meni called from below. I could see that he found me with the beam of his flashlight.

I gained my breath and composure. 'Yes, but I can't come back down and the pieces that I'm standing on are loose. This was an obvious trap for anyone breaking into the repository from the entrance at the top of the stair well.'

'Indeed, Doctor Mane…indeed. Can you go up?'

I flashed my light into the dust-filled stairwell and soon noticed two protruding railings and a number of remaining stairs. I pulled out my rope and tied a quick loop at the end.

'I'm going to try to get a rope on the railings above and go up.' I swung the rope with difficulty due to being close to the wall. After several attempts, it latched onto the railing on the right wall.

'OK…I'm going to swing out and pull myself up onto the stairs…then go through the door at the top. Take this and wait there…if need be, you know the way out.' I threw down my machete and other items to him.

'Careful, Doctor Mane…I will be fine.' He replied.

I swung out and pulled myself up the five feet of rope and onto the first step. I stood up and found the remaining stairs to be solid.

'Looks good from here!' I yelled down the stairwell. Just as I did, the door above me opened and the light revealed the outline of several men….one obviously Marxum. I ran up the steps towards the group and hoped to use my former running back skills to weave my way through them. Successful at first, a timely placed trip sent me flying, and that was the last thing I could remember is Marxum saying something related to, "Aten – the Sun god awaits you."

CHAPTER 11

Jackpot

M Y EYES CLOSED, I woke with a pounding headache in sweltering heat. The light in front of me was so bright I couldn't open my eyes. I turned my head to the side to avoid the light and could see that my hands were bound to a stakes on either side of me…as were my feet. I was apparently left in the middle of a desolate area, tied to stakes in the scorching sun.

This was an obvious move by Marxum, as I now faced the Sun god, the Aten, literally face-to-face. I struggled with the ropes tied to my ankles and wrists and was able to free my right foot…not that that helped, but it gave me hope. My mouth was parched and all I could think of was a tall, cold glass of water. The heat exhausted me quickly and I closed my eyes and tried to rest to regain my strength. I would try again in a little while.

I must have dozed for the next thing I heard was murmured voices. I was dreaming and I stood before my archaeology class at the university with the beautiful Cathedral of Learning in view on a crystal clear day. I was reading off a homework assignment to the class and the murmur of the students rustling appeared almost live. 'Professor! Professor!'

In my delirium, I looked to my left and right trying to catch a glimpse of the student that was calling me. All I felt was the unbearable heat and squinted heavily attempting to open my eyes to my beckoning student.

'Professor! Can you hear me?' Came the voice again. Someone was working around my wrists and placing something wet on my forehead. 'Can you hear me?'

'Yeah…yeah…' I murmured.

'It's me, Professor….Teddy.' Came the voice of my student.

'Who?? Waterhouse??…' My senses were coming back slightly.

'Yes..yes…it's me. I'm going to pour you some water.'

'I'm not changing your grade, Waterhouse...I don't care how much you try to brown nose.' I replied in a slurred, delusional voice.

'Huh? Sun has gotten to you, but have some water and it'll help.' I felt a cup coming to my lips and inhaled the glorious liquid. 'Slow, Professor... drink it slow.' I was soon sitting and thanked Waterhouse for showing up when he did. He mentioned that he hid from Marxum's men after they went into the palace basement. When he overheard that they had tied me up in the sun, he came as soon as he had an opportunity. 'You know me, Professor...always where the action is...saving the day.' For once, he was right...but, only this once.

We headed for my vehicle, which Waterhouse had used to reach me. I could walk, but with difficulty due to my legs cramping. 'I also sent a message to the museum director, Professor, and to the U.S. embassy... thought that they needed to know what was happening.'

'The embassy? You contacted the embassy, Waterhouse??'

'Yes, we may need some protection down here and I thought they would be the most sympathetic.' He answered emphatically.

'You know what that means, don't you? Contacting the embassy?' I tried to get him to look me in the eye.

'No...not really...what's the deal?'

'You know who they're going to send to investigate?' I answered perturbed to an extent.

'No, who?' he answered as we continued to walk.

'Miss Liza Kertis, that's who?'

'Oh! Well, Professor, maybe I did a good thing then.' He smirked and brushed back his hair. 'I think she has a thing for me...I don't blame her.'

I shook my head. 'I didn't want to have her bail us out again, Waterhouse. We're supposed to be self-sufficient.'

'She'll probably run right down here...now that she knows I put in the call.' Waterhouse answered with continued hair stroking.

'Maybe that'll actually have her send someone else.' I murmured.

We got into the vehicle and continued the discussion all the way back to my dig site. I was in no position to drive, so I let Waterhouse take the wheel. Considering that he somehow had already lost a wheel from another vehicle in the past few weeks...I wasn't certain that I was safer now than an hour ago. We needed to get back to the site to find Dr. Meni, since neither of us knew his whereabouts.

'I was told they'd left for the day, Professor.' Waterhouse started as he slowly pulled up to the site. 'They figured that they had the situation under control and would return in the morning to begin their exploration of the basement.'

'We go back in tonight then.' I said as I slowly crawled from my seat.

'You're in no shape to be going back in there, Professor. Maybe we should find Dr. Meni and go back into town...bring the authorities when we come back.'

'No time, Waterhouse.' I replied walking towards the entrance. 'If they get here before us and find the artifacts, we'll never see them again. I'm going back in...if you prefer to stay out here it could be a good idea. Get a good view of the road coming in and if you see their caravan coming back, let us know. There are some supplies in the back of the truck...I'm going to load up with a some and head in, but first, I need some food, water and a little rest.'

'Your crossbow and weapons? You may need them.' Waterhouse answered while searching the back of the vehicle.

'I dropped them down to Dr. Meni when it looked like I was about to be captured at the top of the stairway.' I replied loading a satchel. 'I need some arrows and ammo, so I'll take them now. Here,' I handed him a machete and Bowie knife. 'Hope you won't need to use them.' We sat in the shade and, while resting, grabbed a quick bite to eat. Soon after, I gave Waterhouse more instructions and headed in.

With renewed energy and adrenaline, I made good time moving through the tunnel. I carried a torch in one hand and flashlight in the other and called out to Dr. Meni.

I called Dr. Meni's name over and over and it echoed heavily in the cavernous hallways. I didn't receive a reply, but also didn't believe that Marxum's men had taken him. They didn't want to take a chance at angering the Egyptian government any more than they already had and Water boy never mentioned that Marxum's men had gone back into the palace. Besides, they had me and that's all that Marxum actually cared about.

Finally, after fifteen minutes of calling his name, I heard a faint response and moved in that direction. I was again in the passage way that Dr. Meni and I had discovered earlier in the day. Surprisingly, it appeared that he performed a stratification of the site and had continued with the search even after I had been taken. Not that I had a problem with that, considering if someone was to find the crown, I would prefer it would be someone on my team.

I heard his faint call again. 'This way.'

I rushed through the columned hall and soon saw the staircase that I had attempted to climb. I could see a torch light through an open door that appeared to have been exposed when the staircase collapsed.

'Dr. Meni…I'm here!' I yelled through the door.

'I'm here, Doctor…I'm here.' Came the reply.

I stuck my torch through the door and noticed a large room. At its center was what appeared to be a throne on a pedestal with two lit torches on either side. Seated on the throne was Dr. Meni.

'Dr. Meni…What is this place?' I asked as my eyes wondered the heavily adorned walls.

'It is the treasury room…of the Pharaoh Akhenaten.' He replied with a stern expressionless face.

'This is it! This is what we've been searching for!' I said as I approached the room's center. 'We found it. Tell me, Doctor, what you wear on your head….is it…?'

He looked right at me, though, still with an expressionless face. 'It is the Double-crown of Egypt…at least…what remains of it.' His expression still did not change and his voice was methodical and, I must admit, eerie.

I analyzed it from about five feet away. 'It's the frame of the Double-crown…' I said. 'I can see it…it's the frame of the crown. It was made of material with a wire frame…the material deteriorated as I expected.'

'Admire it, Dr. Mane…but, it belongs to Egypt. You cannot have it to take to some museum in the west.' His head never moved while he spoke and his tone was very stern. His actions were very unlike the Dr. Meni I was familiar with.

'Of course,' I replied hesitantly. 'I had no intention of taking it out of Egypt. You know my methods, Doctor.'

He looked at me intently with eyes that appeared to be glazed. 'People change...I will not allow that to happen. This is my heritage...he was our pharaoh.'

It became apparent that the crown was affecting Dr. Meni in some manner. He continued to sit on the throne almost motionless, except for the movement of his lips.

'You need not worry, Doctor.' I finally replied. 'You have my word.'

'I will hold you to that.' He replied

I turned and looked behind me. 'It's important that we leave now, Doctor. Marxum and his men could return at any time. They will certainly take the crown.'

'Silence! You dare remove me from my throne!' He responded in a loud voice that echoed far into the adjoining hall. It was now very apparent that the crown held some effect on its wearer.

'Dr. Meni,...if you value the crown and would like to preserve it for Egypt...I recommend that we leave now and secure it.' He didn't respond.

I heard a faint calling of my name from a great distance and assumed that it was Waterhouse. If he's coming down here it could mean one of two things...he's afraid to stay outside by himself or...Marxum was on his way. I left the room without saying anything further to Dr. Meni. The name calling became louder and I was now certain it was Waterhouse.

'Professor!! Professor!! Marxum is coming back!' I finally saw him running towards me. 'They are two miles up the road!' He yelled when he caught glimpse of me.

'Okay, Water boy…head back out and start the Jeep…get it ready to go. Have a crate ready too. We'll be up shortly.' I yelled back.

'Okay…will do.' He turned and ran back in the direction of the entrance.

I approached Dr. Meni who still sat motionless on the stone throne. I had no idea how he would react, but I didn't have time to worry about it.

'Dr. Meni, it's urgent that we leave now. Please, follow me…' He did not react to my request, but his lips began to move.

'You ask me to leave my throne!?? Who are you to request such?'

The crown was definitely affecting him, though I had no explanation for it. I now realized that I had no choice but to make my move. I quickly lunged at him and took the crown from his head. Dr. Meni screamed at my maneuver, but didn't try to stop me. Once the crown was removed, he collapsed to the ground in horror. I swiftly walked out of the room with the crown, actually, its frame, in hand.

I turned and saw him move to his hand and knees. He shook his head attempting to get his bearings. He looked up and saw me…he smiled as though he had been released from a spell…a spell of the Pharaoh Akhenaten. He began to apologize, but I stopped him and said we have to leave. We gathered up the supplies and my weapons and headed for the exit. We made it out into the bright sunlight and quickly found Waterhouse standing in the Jeep with binoculars in hand. He turned and excitedly approached us.

'Professor…' he said running towards us. 'They're about a half-mile from here. Luckily, they stopped for a few minutes as soon as they entered the site or else they would have been here already. I would have had to take them all on myself.' He brushed his outfit and confidently adjusted his hat.

'Good thing we showed up, Water boy. Let's pack this crown in the crate and get out of here.'

Within minutes, we were on our way and attempted to weave through the ruins until we could make a run for the main road. We hadn't yet encountered the Marxum vehicles, which Waterhouse mentioned as being three in number, but the site narrowed and we were certain that we would be seen before our exit. I stopped the Jeep at the last point of cover. I waited for a few minutes and informed the others to brace for a sprint to the main road. I leaned on the pedal and threw sand some 20 feet behind us as the Jeep accelerated at full speed. Within minutes, the Marxum vehicles were visible and heading towards us. I had no intention of stopping and they had no idea of who was approaching them. I pulled my revolver and drove with it in one hand. I told Dr. Meni and Waterhouse to find my crossbow and load it.

The Marxum vehicles approached us at a slower pace. They appeared as though they were unsure of what to do about the speeding Jeep that was about to pass them. They didn't react until I was within twenty feet of the lead vehicle. I could see that they recognized me and/or Waterhouse and began to move the lead truck in the path of the Jeep. I drove right around them and kept moving forward, passing the second vehicle, a Jeep carrying Marxum, without incident. By the time we moved up on the third vehicle, they were reaching for weapons. As I drove past, I fired a shot into the back tire of the Jeep and they spun out of control.

We were now heading full speed for the main road and the rear view mirror revealed that the other two vehicles had turned and were in pursuit. I leaned on the pedal and didn't look back until I reached the road. I could see that the Jeep carrying Marxum had passed the lead truck and was moving up on us quickly. Waterhouse mentioned that Marxum's Jeep had a high-powered engine and I could see that our Jeep would soon be overtaken. The occupants of the pursuing Jeep took several shots at our tires, but I began evasive maneuvers and drove in a side-to-side fashion. I yelled to Waterhouse and Dr. Meni to keep their heads down.

The shots being fired at our Jeep weren't connecting, but driving in an erratic fashion to avoid the shots had slowed our pace and Marxum was gaining fast. I was driving and also happened to be the only one in our vehicle that could also handle a weapon with any proficiency. Thus, we were at a significant disadvantage. Marxum, surprisingly, had his driver pull up alongside our back bumper. I took advantage of this good fortune and slammed on the brakes. Marxum's Jeep flew past us and I was now able to pull my revolver and headed towards Marxum. His Jeep turned and came back, but they soon found that they were heading into a barrage of shots. They veered off of the road in an attempt to avoid the shots and we drove past their position.

A quick look in my rear view mirror found that the lead truck had now caught up to us and we faced more shots that were being fired by the passenger in the front seat. I leaned on the pedal, since I was sure we could out run the truck, though, I knew that Marxum's Jeep would soon be back in pursuit before we could reach the town. Within minutes, both the truck and the other Jeep were visible in the rear view mirror. To make matters worse, another Jeep could be seen heading directly towards us.

Waterhouse was basically comatose in the front seat and I wasn't even sure he was conscious. Dr. Meni was basically on the floor in the back seat. I pulled my cross bow and waited to see who was coming towards us. As the Jeep approached, I could see that it had one occupant and it was a woman who was driving. She appeared to be concerned about the approaching vehicles and had slowed and moved to the side of the road. As we passed her, I could see that the face was familiar....it was Sulmona!

I waved frantically at her at the last second and she, hesitantly, returned the wave.

All three vehicles passed her and she, instinctively, knew that we were in trouble and she may have even recognized Marxum and turned her vehicle and to give chase. Sulmona was a good shot with her revolver and she began to pepper Marxum's Jeep and the truck with shots from the rear. They began to drive erratically to avoid the shots and I, again, took advantage of the commotion to turn the Jeep and head back towards Marxum. As I did, I drove past the truck and laid an arrow into the truck's passenger.

We had Marxum on the run and they continued on the road towards the village, but his Jeep soon turned back. I waved to Sulmona and turned to follow her in her pursuit. We drove alongside of the truck and we both laid into the tires with shots and arrows that caused it to spin out of control. I then motioned to Sulmona to keep driving directly into the village. Marxum's Jeep was in our path and we each drove to either side of the road to avoid a confrontation. We flew past him without incident, but soon hit rough roads with large bumps that caused the Jeep to fly into the air several times. I had to pull Waterhouse back into the Jeep in one incident, as he almost flew from his seat.

The terrain on the side of the road was extremely volatile with numerous dips and sand mounds that caused the Jeep to jump and land hard several times. When one jump led to the Jeep hitting almost grill first into the ground, I decided to move back onto the road and then head directly for the village.

I pulled out onto to the road and Sulmona soon followed us from the opposite side. My rear view mirror surprisingly didn't reveal that Marxum was still in pursuit. I took advantage of this opportunity and kept heading directly for the village. After Waterhouse had pulled himself out from under the dashboard and Dr. Meni from the floor of the backseat, they gathered themselves and began to drink from their cantines...hoping upon hope that there was something a little stronger that somehow had found itself into the container.

'Yeah…' Waterhouse began. 'We showed them. Marxum will think twice about messing around with us in the future.'

'You spent most of the time under the dashboard, Water boy, and you almost flew out twice.' I replied with a smirk.

'I was getting as closer view of the potential road hazards…that's all.' He replied defensively. His hair was extremely disheveled. 'No average man could have survived that task…I'll have you know.'

'Thanks…' Was all that I could get out without laughing.

'Dr. Mane! Dr. Mane!' Dr. Meni yelled from the backseat. I think that we have a problem!'

I looked at him through the rearview mirror. 'The crate…with the crown….it's gone!' He said as he searched frantically in the backseat.

'Damn it!!' I replied as I slammed my hands on the steering wheel. 'It must have flown out when we hit the rough roads. That's why Marxum gave up the chase. He saw the crate fly out and they picked it up. He knew it would be something of value or else we wouldn't be carrying it.' I shook my head in disgust. 'Nothing we can do now but get back to the hotel and regroup.'

We made it back to the hotel without further incident. We were dejected at the loss of the crown, but we were certain that this story wasn't over. We parked the Jeep and Sulmona pulled in right behind us. We ran towards each other and I lifted her into the air with the joy of seeing her again. We embraced for several minutes and I thanked her for showing up…several times.

At that point, Waterhouse and Dr. Meni walked up behind us. Sulmona took one look at Waterhouse and smacked me across the head. 'Why did you give him my phone number?!!' She said angrily in her strong Italian accent. 'He's always calling, because he's in some kinda trouble."

I just shrugged and smiled. 'Well, you got to see me again, so it was worth it.' She returned the smile.

Waterhouse grunted smugly. 'You know me, Professor….I don't hesitate to circle the wagons, etc., etc….not when lives are on the line.' He took off his hat and brushed his hair back in true John Wayne style.

I just shook my head. 'Just let him have it.' I said to Sulmona. 'Shall we go inside?'

The four of us walked towards the front entrance of the hotel and, as we approached, I could distinctively smell the fragrance of jasmine. I spotted a woman sitting in a large wicker chair on the porch of the hotel. She wore a large hat, sunglasses and a kaki suit. She held a large smile as we approached and waved a newspaper in a cooling motion.

'I see that you managed to make it back on your own, Dr. Mane.' The American accent and the voice were distinctive. 'Saves me from driving all the way out there in this heat.' It was Liza Kertis – U.S. Emissary in Northern Africa.

I chuckled. 'You know, I was wondering when you were going to show up.'

She smiled. 'When I received two calls about the circumstance…I decided I better see what the situation is.'

'Two calls?' I replied as we were all finally on the porch of the hotel.

'Yes…one from the Director of Antiquities and the other from…Miss Confetti here.'

Sulmona shrugged. 'I was worried.'

CHAPTER 12

A Sight for Sore Eyes

T HE GROUP OF US went into the small "restaurant" area of the hotel, where we ordered beverages and small plates of food. Sitting at a long, plank board table, we discussed the predicament that we were in and what course of action to take in order to regain the crown.

'I need some nourishment to get my strength back-up.' Waterhouse said as he sat cockily in his chair. This was his typical demeanor when women were around. 'Working undercover in Marxum's camp took a toll on me...all that dealing in the shadows stuff...counter-espionage work...I need to get my body and mind sharp again.'

'What undercover work were you performing again, Mr. Waterhouse? Did I miss something?' asked Dr. Meni sipping a cold beverage.

'He wasn't doing any undercover work.' I replied quickly.

'In a sense I was!' Waterhouse answered defensively. 'I gained you some important information.'

'You were working for Marxum because he paid you.' I answered.

'OK, guys...' Liza chimed in. 'I need to know more of what we're dealing with here, please.'

'Yes, of course.' I said as I held up my hand to stop Waterhouse from stupidly uttering something else. 'As you are aware, I was commissioned by the Director of Antiquities to search for the most prized and elusive of all ancient Egyptian artifacts...the Double-Crown of Egypt. To make a long story short, I determined that there would be a potential to find the crown here in Amarna.'

'This is where the Pharaoh Akhenaten built his own capital.' Dr. Meni stated.

'Why did the Akhenaten build his own capital? Wasn't the current capital of Thebes sufficient?' Liza asked.

'Akhenaten was the most unique Pharaoh in all of ancient Egypt.' Dr. Meni continued. 'He was known as the "heretic Pharaoh" and made many…unpopular…changes to Egyptian society.'

'Akhenaten's major change…' I replied. 'Was moving from polytheism to monotheism….from the belief of many gods…to the belief of one god. This was first time in history that that happened, but now it is commonplace. Needless to say…his theory in the belief of just one god…the Sun God…was very unpopular.'

'So he builds his own capital here and hides from the masses that are ticked off at him.' Liza replies between sips of her beverage.

'So to speak and it worked for a while.' I continued. 'Upon his passing, many of his statues were destroyed and society attempted to erase him from history. His son, who was now Pharaoh, even converted the Egyptian religion back to polytheism.'

Dr. Meni replied. 'His son, Miss Kertis, was the most well-known Pharaoh in history…the Pharaoh Tutankhamen.'

'King Tut???' Liza replied sitting forward in her chair. 'His son was King Tut??'

'Yes.' I answered. 'Tut also moved the capital back to Thebes and left Amarna to the drifting sands.'

Liza sat back in her seat. 'So, you believed that because Akhenaten's palace was abandoned, there was a good opportunity to find the treasured crown? I'm assuming that there was only one crown.'

'Yes and no.' I replied. 'We do believe that there is only one *true* crown.'

'You said you found a crown, Marshall…' Sulmona said.

'Again, Yes, Dr. Meni did discover a crown, more-so a frame of a crown, in the palace. Though, we don't believe that it is the true crown. We believe that there is only one such crown which was passed down from Pharaoh to Pharaoh.'

'So, *what* crown did you find, Dr. Mane?' Liza asked.

'We didn't find the true crown…we believe that we found the Double-Crown of the Pharaoh Akhenaten.'

Dr. Meni cleared his throat. 'An attempt was made to erase the entire history of Akhenaten and we believe that the crown was purposely left in the abandoned palace so that Akhenaten's legacy would not carry on to future Pharaohs.'

'Basically, we found the second most important crown in ancient Egyptian history.' I answered. 'Now, at this time, we've lost it.'

'So, Dr. Mane,' Liza said while sitting back in her chair. 'What is your plan? I know you always have one.'

I grinned. 'There is only one option the way I see it. We have to get it back…no matter what it takes. I will go to Marxum's camp in the morning and, hopefully, remove it without anyone noticing.'

'That is very dangerous, Doctor.' Dr. Meni stated with a concerned look. 'Let us have the authorities handle it.'

'I appreciate your concern, Doctor.' I stated. 'But, if I know Marxum, he will have the crown out of his camp and on the black market within days. They'll never trace it back to him…he's too sly. No, we have to move as soon as possible and I'll head there in the morning.'

'Then I shall join you.' Dr. Meni replied. 'I have to…it is for my country. This crown must be preserved.'

'I will too.' Liza said. 'I can have some men from the Director's security office here by morning. Marxum is not required to let them into his personal tents, so you may still have to find your way in, while we distract them at the entrance.'

I nodded. 'I appreciate both of your offers. I have to accept them for the sake of the crown.'

'You know you can count on me, Marshall.' Sulmona stated with a smile. 'I have no intention of staying behind.'

Waterhouse sat up cockily in his seat and swirled the drink in glass. He cleared his throat. 'I'm happy that all of you will be joining in this recovery effort. I was going to take care of most of the details of this operation myself…you know…help out the Professor with some stealth work and the like. But, I'll spread the wealth, so to speak. Thanks for volunteering.' He finished with a nod.

'Thanks, Water boy,' I replied just shaking my head. 'Okay, then you and Sulmona will help me search the camp, while Liza and the Director's men cause some confusion at the gate. Dr. Meni, you can be our eyes from the hill above the camp and our getaway driver.'

Everyone agreed and the time was set for the next morning.

CHAPTER 13

Offense is the Best Defense

AT THE STATED TIME the next morning, the entire group found themselves in their positions. Dr. Meni held a position behind heavy brush on a small hill which overlooked the camp. Sulmona, Waterhouse, and I were hidden to his right, but very close to the rope that outlined the perimeter. We could see the kaki clad Dr. Meni, through the dense brush. Our Jeep was positioned about hundred yards back from our location.

Even though we were soon to face danger, Waterhouse tried to play it cool by casually opening and closing a pocket knife. His bugged out eyes told a completely different story.

'Liza and the Director's men should be arriving any minute.' I said while peering through the brush. I checked my revolver and replaced it in the holster. I then loaded the crossbow and slung it across my back. Sulmona already had her revolver in her hand and I motioned to her to put it away. She has a reputation of using the weapon carelessly.

We soon heard the rumble of vehicles approaching and the camp began to slowly stir. We could see a few men move towards the direction of the vehicles, which were approaching from the rear of the camp. I could see the approaching dust clouds of two vehicles, both Jeeps. They came at a normal pace and drove along the left side of the camp right past us. The first Jeep was white and had two rugged looking men inside and then Liza's beige Jeep soon followed. They drove to the front of the camp, but as planned, they continued past the entrance and drove to the other side, circled around back and then past us again. They finally stopped at the entrance.

The camp was really awake at this point and we could see several men exit the tents and head towards the entrance. Liza and the Director's men sat in their vehicles for a minute and exchanged conversation before beginning to slowly exit. This slight delay was to draw more of the camp dwellers towards the front of the camp. They met for a few seconds and then walked towards the entrance.

We immediately looked to Dr. Meni who was watching the scene with binoculars and he clearly gave us the "go-ahead" signal. I looked back at Sulmona and Waterhouse. Sulmona was ready, but I think that Waterhouse was more interested in digging a hole and hiding.

'I'm slipping out first…' I said. 'Bella…cover me and then follow-me in about a minute. Water boy…you follow about thirty-seconds later. We'll convene at the back of that tent to the right.' They both nodded.

We each made our way into the camp at the respective intervals and without incident. Sulmona and I both had our revolvers in hand and I motioned to Waterhouse to keep his machete handy.

I peeked around the corner of the tent and noticed one of the workers moving directly towards us. I waited for him to round the corner and took him out with a forearm across the side of his face. He fell quickly, but quietly. The three of us now moved along the side of the tent and I looked to Waterhouse for direction. He pointed straight ahead and we moved silently in that direction. We came to the entrance of a tent and he motioned that we may want to look inside. I slid in first and found the tent to be empty and then waved for the others to enter.

'This is the supply tent.' Waterhouse said in whispered tones. 'It's possible the crown could be in here.'

'Possible, yes, but not probable.' I replied as my eyes scanned the entire contents of the tent. 'I'm thinking Marxum wouldn't let that out his sight, but it's worth checking. Let's go through this stuff quickly…we have no idea how long Liza can keep them busy. Sulmona, take a quick look through these boxes here at the front and then keep an eye out.'

Sulmona began to open the lids on the boxes closest to the entrance, while Waterhouse and I each took to separate sides of the tent. I met Waterhouse at the back of the tent and neither had found anything of interest. We walked back towards Sulmona who stated that the coast was clear. We moved out, one at a time, and hid between two close tents. We could hear a rather loud, but indiscernible discussion coming from the camp entrance. So far, Liza was working her magic, since there was no one wondering the grounds.

I checked the map of the camp layout and pointed at Marxum's tent. Waterhouse directed us to the right of our location. I told them to hold their position and follow me into the tent in three minutes. I moved out slowly and caught a glimpse of the crowd at the entrance. There was an animated discussion going on, but I couldn't make out any faces. I did hear one of workers state that someone was "unavailable." Could that someone be Marxum and, if so, why not?

I spotted the nicest tent in the camp and it was the same one on the drawing...definitely Marxum's. Instead of going directly into the tent, I decided to circle it in order to listen for movements inside. I approached from the back and then moved along its right side and then left. I could not hear any movement, but I could hear a low murmur coming from inside. I pinned my ear to the tent and could hear the equivalent of a quiet chant. Someone was definitely in the tent.

I drew my crossbow and held it with my left hand, while holding my revolver in my right. As soon as I did, someone walked up behind me and I threw an elbow into their midsection and hit them with the butt of the crossbow as they bent over. Hoping that it wasn't Waterhouse or Sulmona, I was pleased to see that it was one of Marxum's men who apparently just stumbled their way in that direction.

I moved swiftly towards the front of the tent and didn't hesitate to go through the opening. What I saw was a complete surprise. Marxum sat in a large chair at the center of the tent with two torches on either side and two of his men were kneeling on either side of the chair. Marxum eyes were transfixed as though he didn't notice my entrance. On his head...he wore the frame of the double-crown of Akhenaten.

The chant came from the two men on either side of Marxum and my entrance startled them. The chant stopped and they rose from their position, holding swords, and preparing to attack.

'Okay, Marxum, just give me the crown and no one gets hurt.' I said as I pointed my weapons in their direction. 'You know that I can take them down easily.'

His eyes, which still hadn't looked in my direction, slowly moved towards me. 'Silence!' he said loudly. 'How dare you come in here?' He seemingly spoke in a slow and methodical manner, similar to Dr. Meni when I found him wearing the crown.

'Enough of the charades, Marxum…just hand me the crown and we all walk out of here. There is no way out.' At that moment, Sulmona entered the tent with her revolver pulled and Waterhouse followed. 'As you can see, the odds are getting worse for you by the minute and we also have government officials at the front gate…let's just make this easy on everyone.'

'You dare tread on my ground?' He answered. 'You will pay for such treachery…' he waved his hand towards his two men. One began to very slowly edge his way in our direction, while the other lifted his sword and swung it at a nearby rope, slicing it easily.

I took aim at the man approaching with my crossbow, but the three of us were overwhelmed by a net that dropped from the roof of the tent. The net was heavy and thick and its weight began to drag us to the ground. I fired off an arrow as I went down that easily cut through the net, but the shot went wayward. At the same time that the net dropped, the back of the tent pulled open in unison. The two men carried Marxum through the back of the tent and were quickly out of sight.

I pulled my knife and began to cut at the netting, which surprisingly sliced easily. Sulmona lifted the netting to help with the process and we were soon able to slip through a large enough slit. Waterhouse, who I've accused of having difficulty finding his way out of paper bag, didn't quite find the same hole and struggled like a fish caught in the netting. We finally pulled the netting off of him and ran through the back of the tent. Marxum was gone for the moment. We then moved towards the entrance of the camp where we could see that Liza and the Director's men were getting into a heated discussion with some of the more unsavory of men that belonged to Marxum's group.

Once the three of us came up on Marxum's men from the rear, the situation calmed and they backed down. The Director's men ordered all of them into the nearest tent. A Jeep pulled up in front of the entrance and we ran out to find Dr. Meni arriving in our Jeep with two local law officials. The local authorities took control of the situation and stated that they would hold Marxum's men in the tent.

Fallory, the archaeologist who was working with Marxum, asked to step out of the tent to speak to us. He stated that he was in disagreement with Marxum's actions and that we may be able to find him back at the palace site. Fallory stated that he was aware of a car that was hidden some one-hundred yards from camp that Marxum had mentioned was for "emergencies."

CHAPTER 14

The Palace of Pain

W E RAN OUT TO the Jeeps and were soon on our way. I drove with Sulmona and Waterhouse in my Jeep, Liza and Dr. Meni were in the second vehicle and the Director's men followed in theirs. We didn't encounter Marxum and his men on our way and we pulled up to my dig site without incident.

We gathered in some shade and I addressed the small group.

'I noticed some car tire tracks coming into this area about a quarter mile back. They went towards the north, which would be where Marxum had his dig site. We can reasonably assume that it's him. It's best that we walk there…it's not far…we'll have a better chance of surprising him.'

'He only has two men with him…is that correct Dr. Mane?' Asked one of the Director's men, whose name I still didn't know.

'That's how many he left with, so there are least two.' I replied while adjusting my fedora. 'They'll do just about anything to get away…that's Marxum's reputation, so stay on your guard.'

We began to walk in the direction of Marxum's dig site on what was now a hot, bright, sweltering day in the desert. Dr. Meni walked up along my side.

'I was wondering when you would be interested in talking.' I said with a slight smile. 'You heard what happened back there, I assume?'

'Yes, Sulmona explained the incident in Marxum's tent.' He answered sternly.

'Interesting…isn't it?' I said. 'You are the only one who can explain what happens when that crown is worn, since you experienced it.'

'I did, but it's not easy to explain.' He said while wiping his brow. 'It's as though you are in another world. It's almost as though it's ancient Egypt again…as an Egyptologist…it's incredible, you don't want to take it off. You're there, Doctor Mane, you're there…at the time of Akhenaten's reign.'

I looked at him. 'Is it Akhenaten…is it him speaking to you?'

He shook his shoulders. 'I felt a presence…someone was speaking through me. I could control it to some extent…then again, I couldn't. It may have been him, it was his crown…we were in his palace…'

'Pharaohs were considered "gods," but we know that to be mere interpretation.' I answered. 'Akhenaten was very unique, different from any pharaoh before or after him…do you have a theory?'

He slightly shook his head. 'Let's review his history. Akhenaten was one of the most controversial Pharaohs to rule Egypt. According to Egyptian mythology, he descended from the gods who arrived on Earth at the time of Tep Zepi. People still believe that this Pharaoh did, in fact, come from the stars.

'He came to reign in 1352 BC, and ascended to the throne as the tenth pharaoh of the 18th dynasty. Almost immediately, he instituted a series of radical religious changes, including a ban on references to multiple gods. He abandoned traditional Egyptian polytheism and introduced the worship of the Aten – the sun god. An early inscription likens him to the sun, again from the sky, and the only emblem he allowed was a sun emblem, literally a sun disk with curious arms or rays pointing down. Akhenaten claimed to be a direct descendant of Aten and, like any other pharaoh, Akhenaten regarded himself to be divine, he was a god, but not only did he believe himself to be a god, the whole nation saw him as a god and worshiped him like one.'

Dr. Meni glanced at me with uneasiness. 'You know, according to writings by Akhenaten and poems that were written about him in later years, he was visited by beings that descended from the sky, who told Akhenaten what he needed to do, and perhaps this is why he removed all other symbols of other gods from Egypt and implemented his changes. His appearance was also unusual, which added to the theory. He had an elongated skull, long neck, sunken eyes, thick thighs, long fingers, backward-turned knee joints, a prominent belly that suggests pregnancy and female-like breasts. The first thing that is strange is his elongated skull, and in all of the statues and depictions of him, we see this elongated skull. In general, his body was sort of like a feminine and masculine mixture. This was totally opposite to the idealized iconography of traditional Egyptian artists that showed these big and strong looking Pharaohs.

Why would he make changes in the royal iconography to show him as this "weak" Pharaoh? His wife, Nefertiti, was also depicted as having an elongated skull, did they have some kind of genetic anomaly that caused their heads– and body's in general to be misshaped and disproportional?

In 1907, the actual body of Akhenaten was discovered in Egypt's Valley of the Kings by British archaeologist named Edward Ayrton. After unearthing Akhenaten's mummified remains, Edward Ayrton was able to confirm that the ancient pharaoh's skull was misshapen and elongated. Akhenaten was succeeded by his son, Tutankhamun, who became the most renowned pharaoh of all time. When his tomb was discovered in 1922 by Howard Carter, Tutankhamun was also found to have an elongated skull.'

'What are you saying Doctor?' I said as I almost came to a complete stop. 'You're describing someone who may not be from this world. I'm obviously aware of the oddities of Akhenaten and the mysteries that surround him, but you seem to be implying there is even more to the story.'

He slowed for a moment, glanced at me, and then continued his pace. 'The theories surrounding Akhenaten have always led to such speculation...though very veiled. I don't believe that anyone would stake their reputation on that aspect of his history.'

I shook my head. 'You think enough of it to bring it up, Doctor. Any particular reason?'

He smiled. 'Maybe it was the experience with the crown that made me consider it in a different light. I'm not certain. I think that we should be wary of the theory and what affect the crown will have on a mind…a somewhat already bizarre mind…of Marxum.'

We reached Marxum's dig area and, as expected, a black car sat hidden behind several wall remnants. I held up my hand for the group to stop and then motioned for them to spread out and look for sight of Marxum or others. They were to report back in five minutes. At the specified time, everyone returned with no sightings noted. Marxum was inside his dig site, which was a tunnel that he created in an attempt to reach the lower level of Akhenaten's palace.

I told the group to be on the alert, since we were going in. The seven of us entered the tunnel with three flashlights and a torch as our only light. We were fully aware that the lights would give us away well before we were sighted. With pistols drawn, the Director's men and I led the group, followed by Liza, Dr. Meni and Waterhouse. Sulmona covered the rear.

It was a brief trek before we reached the end of the tunnel. The tunnel led to a recently discovered doorway that apparently led into the palace. Waterhouse stated that they were looking for this doorway when he was part of Marxum's team, but he left the dig before they found it. He mentioned that Marxum was looking for this door, but he never told them what he expected to find inside the palace.

I took the torch and shined it through the doorway. The light didn't carry far and I couldn't see more than about ten yards. I walked in and then waved in one of the Director's men, whose name I just learned was Anwar, and the other one was Shir. We walked slightly further into the darkness and noticed another passage way. I called for the rest of the group to enter and we went directly into the passage, which was a well-paved and adorned hallway within the palace.

The entire hallway was filled with hieroglyphs depicting the adoration of the Sun god, Aten. I stopped to read the glyphs and was soon joined by Sulmona and Waterhouse.

'This is a passage to a temple.' I said as I waved the torch from right to left across the hieroglyphs. 'The hieroglyphs are very clear…Marxum must have found the temple of Aten.'

'Yes, Marshall, it's the Aten that is shown…the only god for Akhenaten.' Sulmona replied as her eyes scanned the glyphs in unison with her flashlight.

'He didn't say that what we were looking for, but it's obvious he had a plan that didn't include his team.' Waterhouse said.

I headed back to the front of the group and we kept moving. The smell of a torch soon hit me and it was apparent that someone had recently passed through this area. We moved cautiously, but briskly and came upon yet another doorway. The door was closed and we stopped to ponder the situation. Recollections of similar situations in World War II brought back my Captain Mane inclinations.

I addressed the group. 'Sulmona…you and Anwar lay on the ground with pistols drawn and aimed at the doorway. When I open the door… fire at anything that moves in there. Shir and I will slip in if there is no activity. Liza…Water boy…Dr. Meni…stay against the wall…when that door opens…hit the room with light…flashlights and torch light.

With everyone in position, I slowly opened the door. We hit the entrance with lights, but no activity was immediately noticed, but we did notice that there was a light in the distance.

'Okay, let's go, Shir. Cover us…and then follow us in.' I said to the group.

We slid into the room on each side of the door. We could see the light emanating from a far corner of what appeared to be an enormous room. We moved closer to the light in a much protected manner. We could hear the rest of the group slowly entering behind us.

We kept silent to not attract attention, but the lights that we carried would do the talking for us. As we approached, I could see the light more clearly, but it was a hazy light and nothing could be discerned. Our proximity made it much clearer that the light was high above us at the far end of the room. The room must have been cavernous, since our slow footsteps echoed heavily and our flashlights couldn't find walls.

Suddenly, we heard a rumble in the direction of the light and more light began to appear. The light ascended like the rising of the sun from the east. The group stopped and I told them to spread out and to douse the lights. The light continued to slowly expand and it soon became apparent that an exterior wall was opening and exposing the sweltering sun. The light increased and the wall continued to rise from what appeared to be fifty yards away and equally that high from ground level.

As the wall rose and the light fashioned the background, I could see the outline of a figure standing directly in the middle on the high ledge. Two other men were in close proximity and it was obviously Marxum. As our eyes adjusted to the brightness, I could see the figure in the middle wearing what appeared to be something on his head. Marxum was still wearing the crown of Akhenaten. The wall stopped rising after it had created a large opening to the sky.

We were no longer under the cover of darkness, since the light carried throughout the enormous room, which was now entirely visible.

'Marshall,' Sulmona quietly stated. 'We're in the temple of Aten.'

There was no doubt. It was elaborately adorned with statues and hieroglyphs of the Aten and in a great state of preservation. At the far end of the room where the light emanated, stood a large altar. The altar was below the wall that had just moved. I nodded and looked back to the light. 'Marxum! You're here…we're here…come down and let's talk this through. You have made a great discovery in finding this temple… let's not ruin the moment.'

There was no immediate response. Marxum stood stoically in front of the open sky that was his backdrop. He slowly raised his hand and began to chant. The two men on either side of him knelt and also joined in. It was obvious that the effect of the crown still had a hold of his actions. With Marxum, it didn't take much for him to be involved in something sinister and the crown appeared to be adding to his personality trait.

He stopped the chant and began to speak. 'You have entered the temple of the Aten…you are not worthy. Only three in your group are…the native people of this great land. Only they may approach the altar.'

I looked to Dr. Meni and the Director's men. They returned my gaze and I nodded. 'This could be our best chance to get close.' I said. 'Anwar, Shir…be ready. Dr. Meni…stay behind them. We'll cover you from here.'

The three of them nodded and slowly began to walk in the direction of the altar. They reached the altar and stood looking up towards the light. Dr. Meni's head swiveled in several directions, as he absorbed the archaeological greatness of his surroundings.

Marxum raised his hand again and the chant started once more. 'He's crazy, Professor.' Waterhouse said trying to stop his knees from shaking. 'I think we ought to slowly back out of here and regroup.'

'We need to deal with this now.' Liza said without taking her eyes from Marxum. 'If not, Marxum may just disappear again.'

A rumble again could be heard. The figures at the top of the ledge didn't move and they continued to chant louder. We all looked around and I could see the three men at the altar hunker down in their position. A large stone pillar rose from behind Marxum. The scraping of limestone against limestone was loud and grinding. The pillar finally stopped some twenty yards above Marxum's head. He continued to chant louder and the two men on either side of him rose. The three of them raised both arms into the air. As they did, a large disk atop the pillar swiveled and moved inward towards the inside of the temple. As it slowly swiveled, the intensity of the sun increased with each passing second. I motioned to the group to slowly back away. We were stopped in our tracks by a piercing light which blinded us to the point that we dropped to our knees trying to cover our eyes. It intensified with each second and it was apparent that the sun god was punishing us for entering his temple.

I removed my hands from my eyes and tried to make out what was happening, but it was absolutely blinding. I could see that the light was only directed at the four of us and not the three men in front of the altar. Waterhouse dropped to the ground and covered his head. 'I can't see...I can't see!' He exclaimed in terror.

Liza and Sulmona also were kneeling with their heads covered by both arms. The light not only was bright, but intensely hot. The intensity of both continued to increase and we were prone to its fate. I heard a cry coming from my right and tried to look in that direction. Sulmona's blouse was on fire and she desperately attempted to douse it with one hand, while the other still covered her eyes. The situation was getting dire and I could hear the calls of Dr. Meni and the Director's men yelling to Marxum to stop his actions. As soon as they did, the disk adjusted and flooded the altar area also. They dropped to their knees to avoid the intensity of the light.

I forced myself to my feet and moved as far to my left as possible. I found a small stone table and hid behind it. I called to everyone in the room to move from their location and to find cover. The filtering of the light from behind the table was a god send of another kind. I used the table as a screen and slightly peaked around the edge and towards the disk. It was an enormous mirror that was reflecting the overly intense desert sun at the ultimate angles. This was the sun god entering his temple…and we were in his way.

Just as I was about to move back behind the glorious shade of the table, I could see Anwar, Shir, and Dr. Meni climbing a set of stairs to the far right of the room. They were apparently heading for the ledge. I looked to my right to see the whereabouts of Sulmona, Waterhouse and Liza. Sulmona, whose blouse fire was out, hid behind a statue of the sun god, while Waterhouse still lay prone in the middle of the room and apparently in a full panic. I could barely make it out, but Liza was slowly crawling in my direction and she had tied her scarf around her eyes.

I had dropped my revolver in the first blast of the intense sun light. I pulled my crossbow from across my back and loaded it almost blindly. On my elbows, I again peaked around the table. The overly intense light sent me back for cover. I rubbed my eyes and went back for another attempt. I knew I had just a split second to eye my target. I moved out, opened my eyes to the light, found the approximate target, which was the enormous mirror, and fired. I quickly rolled back behind the table. I noticed that the light continued to penetrate heavily and Waterhouse was not moving in the middle of the room. I loaded the crossbow again and slid out slowly. I opened my eyes and fired. I moved back behind the table and covered my eyes. I heard a large crash of material breaking and falling to the ground and the light dispersed significantly. I lay on my back, closed my eyes and rested for a minute….one glorious minute.

'Doctor Mane, it looks like the intensity of the light has really dropped. Nice shot!' It was Liza who had crawled up behind me.

I opened my eyes to the high and elaborately adorned ceiling above me. 'Thanks, but there was some luck involved…I could barely see a thing. The light has lessened, but it's still reflecting heavily. I know why too.'

'I can actually see…so, that's a big improvement.' She said as she wiped her brow with a handkerchief. 'Look!! They made it the ledge and are going towards Marxum!'

I quickly rolled out from behind the table to see Anwar, Shir, and Dr. Meni heading towards Marxum's position. Marxum hadn't moved, even with the destruction of the mirror. The two men that were with Marxum both drew swords and a bad confrontation was about to happen. I loaded the crossbow and fired off a shot, taking down the closer of the two men with a heavy impact. Shir fired off a shot at the other man, but it didn't faze him and he ran directly towards them with vengeance. Anwar came up along his side and threw a shoulder into him, which caused him to fall heavily and causing the sword to fall over the ledge and crash loudly on top of the altar below. The Director's men then both jumped on him and he was subdued.

Dr. Meni, who was behind both Anwar and Shir, surprising began to run at full speed towards Marxum, who had yet to move. He reached the still stoic Marxum and rammed into him at full speed. Marxum flew several yards to his right and impacted the ground with a heavy force. Dr. Meni had bounced off of Marxum and actually flew backwards, but he achieved his intention…the crown had flown off Marxum's head in the collision and dropped over the ledge. Not so surprisingly…to me, at least…it landed standing up directly in the center of the altar below.

I instructed Liza to check on Waterhouse, who was still prone in the middle of the floor. Sulmona was waving towards us from the other side of the room, which was still bright from the heavy rays of the sun disk. I yelled for her to follow me and I ran towards the staircase and made my way up to the ledge several steps at a time.

I found Anwar and Shir still struggling with one of Marxum's men, but they nodded and I ran past them, but not before instructing them to secure Marxum also. Sulmona reached the ledge and I told her to check on Dr. Meni, at the same time, Anwar passed us and drew a pistol on Marxum as he rose to his knees.

I looked out over the expansive room and could see that the sun disk was still emitting significant rays into the temple. I could see that Liza had been able to get Waterhouse to sit up and was getting him to drink from a canteen, but she still struggled to see and was shielding her eyes. I avoided the large pieces of broken glass that covered the ground and moved to the back of the ledge. There, I searched for and found the wooden lever that apparently would raise and lower the tower the sun disk. I threw my weight into the lever and, after several seconds, the roar of the pillar's movement echoed throughout the temple. The disk adjusted itself on the way down, a marvel in ancient engineering, and the sun rays no longer directly reflected from the disk. The temple gently darkened and the Aten was gone.

CHAPTER 15

Conclusion?

S EVERAL HOURS LATER, WE returned to the small hotel and rested. Anwar and Shir had taken Marxum and his men into custody. We thanked them for their help and bravery, but they returned the sentiment for assisting in finding one of the greatest treasures in their country's history. The crown was in their possession and they headed directly for the Egyptian Museum.

As evening approached and the sun began to set behind the horizon, Sulmona, Waterhouse, Liza, Dr. Meni, and I sat at an outdoor café. Waterhouse sat between Sulmona and Liza, thinking it would please them. They both had an awkward lean to the outside of the table, but he never noticed. Dr. Meni and I sat opposite them.

'Tell me Dr. Mane,' Liza began while swirling her drink. 'What on earth was that mirror made of? The heat and light were so intense.'

I nodded. 'It was the transporter of the sun for the god Aten, an original device from the time of Akhenaten. Mirrors made of glass were not invented until many centuries later. At the time of Akhenaten, they typically were made from obsidian, which is a naturally occurring volcanic glass. At other times, they were made of the brightest copper. This mirror was extremely unique…it was made of the brightest copper, which was shined to maximum capacity. On top of the copper, they laid the obsidian. The intensity that the double materials generated was unimaginable.'

'It was incredible…' Sulmona said. 'I couldn't move…it stopped you in your tracks.'

'It was made to show the power of the Aten…to all of the non-believers, of which, as we know, there were many.' I answered. All non-believers were brought to the temple to be subjected to the Aten…the sun. In all reality, they were experiencing a true event.'

Waterhouse nodded confidently and smirked at both women to each side of him. He sat up confidently in his chair. 'Yeah, after I had noticed the great impact that this device was capable of…I decided to take the brunt myself. You know, spare the rest of you so that you could find a way of shutting it down. I ensured that it focused its impact on me.'

Sulmona grunted. 'That was a great job…of passing out and getting sunburnt like a piece of toast.'

'I know…I know it didn't look like I was doing much, but I willing became the target to free the rest of you up.' He puffed his chest out. 'As you can see…we're all sitting here…Marxum is in custody. Plan came together without a hitch.' He snorted proudly.

'You sun tan with the best of them, Water boy…' I replied with a whimsical look.

During the meal, a courier from the hotel arrived with a telegram. I tipped him and sent him on his way. Everyone was interested in its contents, so I read it aloud,

> *My good friend Dr. Mane,*
>
> *Hope you are doing well. I am writing to ask for your assistance, since I know little of the subject. I have come across information of a relic similar to that which you searched for here in Morocco. I believe you will be very interested. It will not be too difficult of a cross to bear.*
>
> *Please contact me soon.*
>
> *Bascarma*

Bascarma was a curator of a museum in Casablanca, who I worked with a couple of years past. Sulmona and Liza both were familiar with him and his note readily brought out their attention. I folded the note and placed it into my pocket.

I nodded at the group. 'We will not let my good friend Bascarma down.' I said while lifting a glass for a toast. 'I'll let you know what he says… but tonight, I think we will enjoy our incredible view of…the setting of the sun.'

Archaeological Background Information

The Search for the Crowns of Egypt

Several remnants of certain crowns of Egypt have been found, but mostly in deteriorated states. A Double Crown has never been found in any state of preservation. Recordation of searches specifically for crowns or, specifically, the Double-Crown is few and far between. Archaeologists and Egyptologists used tomb excavations as their primary target to find these rare artifacts, but have been largely unsuccessful in finding even traces of an intact crown.

Even in the most intact tomb ever discovered, such as that of the Pharaoh Tutankhamen (King Tut), no crown was discovered. The Tutankhamen tomb did include remnants of the Khat and Seshed-Circlet crowns in various stages of deterioration. The Tutankhamen tomb also included his crook and flail, which were almost always carried when wearing the Double Crown. The crook was a cane with a hooked handle, gold in color or gold plated with bluish bands, possibly made of copper and it symbolized the Pharaoh's rule. The flail was a golden rod with three beaded strands at the top. It was designed to represent a whip to punish the enemies of Egypt.

This leads us to the assumption that the reason that no traces of the Double Crown have ever been found is due to the fact that there was only one Double Crown and it was ceremoniously passed down from Pharaoh to Pharaoh. This is a plausible theory considering that many monarchies have such a tradition.

A great majority of Pharaoh related artifacts seem to imply that they were made for each Pharaoh, but the Double Crown was a one-of-a-kind royal headpiece. The crown was not a personal possession; it was an official State item. The Double Crown could also be considered property of the religious temple, since the Pharaoh is deemed to also be the High Priest.

This being the case, the Double Crown of Egypt is by far the most prestigious and cherished artifact of ancient Egypt....and yet to be found.

Upper and Lower Egypt

In ancient Egypt, these references were important to distinguish between the two lands, which were separate entities before the Dynastic periods. The "upper" and "lower" references are confusing, since they do not refer to "northern" and "southern" Egypt as would be supposed.

The "upper" and "lower" references are in relation to the Nile River, which cuts through the entirety of Egypt. The Nile River is only one of handful of rivers in the world which flow south to north and is the longest of that nature in the world. Since the Nile flows from the south, the "upper" portion of the river is located in southern or "upper" Egypt. In contrast, the river ends in the north or "lower" Egypt.

At 4,160 miles in length (6,670 km), the Nile is longest river in Africa and the world.

The river is often associated with Egypt, but only approximately 22 percent of the River Nile is located in the country. The Nile begins in Burundi (central Africa) and crosses Uganda, Ethiopia and Sudan and empties into the Mediterranean Sea in northern Egypt.

The Nile River was the life source for ancient Egyptians and, basically, their world revolved around it. The river created a fertile green valley across the desert during its yearly flood. The silt from these floods created excellent conditions for farming and it was by the banks of the river that one of the oldest civilizations in the world began. The ancient Egyptians lived and farmed along the Nile, using the soil to produce food for themselves and their animals.

Significance of the Crown

The first area of clarification that must be made is regarding the term "crown" and "headdress." The Egyptians used these terms interchangeably, but they are not the same in form and substance. There were as many as ten types of headdresses used and only one was actually the "crown." The different headdresses or crowns included The Atef Crown, The Two Feathers Crown (Double-Feathers Crown), The Amun Crown, The Cap Crown, The Blue Crown, The Hem hem Crown, The Seshed-Circlet, The Royal Vulture Crown, The Khat and Afnet Headdresses and The Royal Ureaus (Nemes Head-Cloth). A further description of these headdresses and crowns are provided later in this chapter.

Of the "crowns" listed above, none are actually the true Crown of Egypt. Of those listed, the one that is most closely associated with the pharaoh is the Royal Ureaus (Nemes Headcloth), which was made most famous because it was depicted on the golden mask of the Pharaoh Tutankhamen (King Tut).

The original true Crown of Egypt was the White Crown. The White Crown appeared as early as 3,000 BC and is first visualized on the Narmer Palette, which was a mudstone, ceremonial palette owned by one of the first and the unifying ruler of Egypt, Narmer. Narmer is depicted wearing the White Crown on the Narmer Palette.

Narmer, from southern Egypt (aka- The Black Land), is credited with unifying Egypt with the Red Land of the north. Northern Egypt's rulers wore the Red Crown and once the two lands were unified, so were the crowns. The White Crown was worn inside the Red Crown representing the merger. This combined crown was called the Double-Crown or the Crown of Egypt.

Other Notable Crowns of Ancient Egypt

The Blue Crown (Khepresh)

The crown is a tall flanged helmet, made of either painted cloth or leather, with the uraeus and vulture on the brow. It is a common headdress shown either with no pattern or a raised pattern of golden circlets.

The first appearance of this crown is depicted on the royal statue of Amenhotep III, with the first true representation shown during the reign of the Pharaoh Kamose. The Blue Crown was first known to have been worn at a point during the Second Intermediate Period to the New Kingdom's 18th Dynasty. At times, the Blue Crown is referred to as the War Crown, but that is not its true intention. It was also worn during hunting expeditions. The most famous depiction of the crown is from a famous painting of Rameses II after his victory over the Hittites.

The Two Feathers Crown

Typically a crown adorned with two ostrich feathers, though falcon feathers were also known to be used, combined with ram horns, disks and a uraei. This crown was known as swty (two feathers) in Ancient Egyptian and was also often referred to as the Double Feathers Crown.

As a royal crown or headdress, it held significance related to the Pharaoh's accession to the throne and was worn during his coronation. The Two Feathers Crown was also often depicted on the gods Montu, Min, Anedjti and Amun. The first appearance of the crown came during the reign of Sneferu in the 4th Dynasty.

The Atef Crown

Similar to the Amun crown, the Atef crown also consisted of two feathers (typically ostrich) and was primarily associated with a highly regarded, ancient Egyptian God, Osiris (the god of rebirth). The crown was elongated, white and also had a gold disk at its top. The crown was primarily used in religious ceremonies.

Hemhem Crown (hmhm)

Worn during very important ceremonies, the Hem Hem Crown is also called the Triple atef Crown, since it resembles an ensemble of three atef crowns, but much more elaborately constructed and decorated. It is most often depicted under the rule of the Ptolemy's, but has been known to exist from the Amarna period during the 18th dynasty. The very first appearance of the Hem hem was an image on an Amarna tomb wall of the heretic pharaoh Akhenaten wearing the crown. The crown is also depicted on the famous gilded throne of Tutankhamen, showing the pharaoh wearing the crown. The Hem hem Crown has meaning in the form of a rising sun, which can be interpreted as a rebirth.

Amun Crown

The Amun crown is always depicted on one of the most prevalent ancient Egyptian god's, Amun and became very popular during the famous 18th dynasty. The crown is known for its two large feathers, which are anchored by a flat base. Variations in the crown's design have also shown the presence of a uraei, horns and even disks. The Amun crown is often worn by the pharaoh, which calls for the god's protection when worn. The crown was worn with or without the feathers and occasionally was worn in this fashion by queens.

Royal Vulture

Worn as a protection from the goddess Nekhbet, the Royal Vulture Crown is the depiction of a flying vulture with wings spread, thus protecting the pharaoh from his enemies.

Cap Crown (sdn)

Typically blue, gold or white linen, the Cap Crown has been depicted with or without decoration. When decorations are depicted they show one or two uraeus, circles or lines, faience beads and embroidery. One of the oldest known crowns, the Cap Crown is represented from the Old Kingdom and still depicted in the 25th dynasty and even their successors. The crown was worn also by Queen Nefertiti during the Amarna period and the only surviving Cap Crown was found on Tutankhamen. The crown was also called the Kushite cap, which was more of a plain version of the Cap crown, and was often depicted on the god Ptah.

The Nemes

The Nemes is one of the most depicted headdresses in all of ancient Egypt. The two colored, striped head-cloth covers the head, neck and shoulders. It was made most famous during the 18th Dynasty by the golden mask of Pharaoh Tutankhamen or King Tut. The Nemes, also called the Royal Ureasus Crown, is a head-cloth and not necessarily a crown, yet it is worn almost exclusively by the Pharaoh or royalty. The Nemes dates back as far as the 3rd Dynasty, in particular, during the time of King Djoser (the first Pharaoh to construct a pyramid). During the 18th Dynasty, it began to be worn together with other crowns. One of the main features of the Nemes was always the uraeus (serpent) attached to the front-center of the cloth. The Nemes is typically worn with a menit, which is pectoral decoration covering the shoulders and chest.

Khat or Afnet Headdresses

Another head-cloth, or what are sometimes referred to as "kerchiefs," are the Khat or Afnet Headdresses. These headdresses are often worn together and they are also dated as far back as the 3rd Dynasty and King Djoser, but there is evidence that it first appeared as far back as the time of King Den. The Khat and Afnet cover the head and neck and are often depicted as a one-colored, typically gold, and a including a uraeus over the forehead. Queens often wore this headdress also, which was very prevalent during the Amarna period.

Seshed Circlet (ssd-mdh)

Often combined with the Double-Feathers or Atef Crowns, the Seshed-Circlet's primary purpose is hold the uraeus and it is attached to base of the other crowns. The Circlet is also worn individually, typically worn with a short wig, and is made of either silver or gold with precious stones (even semi-precious and colored glass) attached.

Crowns of Queens/Royal Women

The ancient Egyptian queens often wore some of the same crowns as the pharaohs. In particular, the Amun, Cap, Seshed Circlet and Khat (Afnet) crowns were known to have been worn by various queens. Of course, if you consider Hatshepsut, the first female pharaoh, a woman has worn all of the crowns mentioned above.

It is said that the most commonly worn crown of the royal women would be the Vulture Cap. This cap evoked the maternal aspect of the queen and was typically associated with the goddess Nekhbet. Another crown commonly worn since the 13th Dynasty was the Double Feathers headdress. Egyptian queens were also known to wear a form of a double or triple Nemes headdress.

ABOUT THE AUTHOR

Rock DiLisio is a freelance writer from Pittsburgh, Pennsylvania, who has an avid interest in archaeology. He is a member of the Archaeological Institute of America and holds certificates in archaeology from the University of Chicago's Oriental Institute and the U.S. Department of the Interior. He is the author of Archaeology-In Brief (Ancient Egypt) and has written other history-related books, such as Firings From the Foxhole (WWII), American Advance (French and Indian War), as well as the travel guide, Italy Central.

His fictional archaeology series includes: Three Kings of Casablanca, Stone of the Sahara and Palace of the Pharaoh. He is also the author of Sherlock Holmes: Mysteries of the Victorian Era and his work has also appeared in magazines, newspapers and periodicals.